Ch
Graceland

For my precious family
and to J.G. Ballard for his friendship and advice

Chasing Graceland

VERNON HOPKINS

Right Publishing

Published by Right Books
85 Great Portland Street
First Floor
London W1W 7LT

ISBN 9781842260364

Contents

One

IN THE GHETTO

Memphis, 1956. Another day, another dawn, another sun blistering the horizon threatening with no sense of urgency but with cold-hearted intentions, telling the population of Memphis to make the most of the few precious hours ahead of them when another groundhog day of sweat, tempers, tantrums and tears kicked in. The weather, oven-hot hazy every single day, tested everyone's patience.

On the poor side of the rambling city where air-conditioning units were as visible as finding a dollar bill in the gutter, the dozen stray dogs and cats foraged into piled up rubbish, due to a lack of workforce affected by the recession-hit county and its downright heatwave lethargy. Seeking out anything edible with their cracked, dried noses, whether it be rotting shock-eyed fish heads buzzing with pregnant bluebottles or other disgusting produce that would make a vulture vomit. It was all eagerly devoured ravenously, later dispensed as poisonous liquid excrement on the same alleyways and streets they lived and died on. Emaciated bodies flopping down anywhere where there was salvation to be found beneath cars, shadowed doorways and below trees. Anywhere, than being sacrificed by a sizzling sun.

Teenage black-American Willard Henderson, asleep in his sparsely-furnished bedroom on the third floor of the run-down tenement building, was perspiring like he was living a lousy dream, one long leg hanging over the side of the threadbare mattress, his other draped over the other side. 6ft 4ins tall and weighing seventeen stone, the single mattress was almost hidden by his frame. Stirred by the irritating sound of the alarm clock vibrating on the bare floorboards, he groaned his way into consciousness as the clock's spring wound down to an ominous 'ting'.

'Die, you bastard,' he yawned, dragging his weary body over the side of the bed, the room demonstrating its size when Willard stood to his full height, stretching, making it seem infinitely smaller than it already was. The rickety fan resting on the tiny bedside table sounded like it needed greasing, no match for the heat still radiating through the thin walls of the tenement, the remnants of yesterday's fierce sun.

Standing there, with a hangdog expression on his face, only too aware of the sweat-laden work ahead of him, had he known how his day would unfold, the look on his 19-year-old face would have turned into fear and desperation. Half-heartedly sliding into his denim jeans he tucked in his grey working shirt, the motive, CHESS AUTOS on its back. Scratching his head, he suddenly heard his mother's plaintive voice calling from her bedroom.

Sadie, bedridden after suffering a stroke and cared for by her son, her only offspring, croaked, 'Willard, you're late again. If you lose that job we're in deep trouble, boy.'

Willard knew what those words meant. Destitution. Entering her darkened bedroom, its bedbound stuffiness caused Willard to open the curtains to the open window. Rising sun bathed the room with stark delivery, showing Sadie propped up with pillows, frail and understandably miserable considering the only time she left her sick bed was to struggle painfully to the toilet and back again.

Willard stood at the open window, gazing down at the almost deserted street below. What with the heatwave and most of the neighbourhood still asleep, having no work to go to, the sight was an indication of the three mile walk ahead of him from the the city limits into town where the showroom stood.

Sadie scolded, 'Don't just stand there son. Get some breakfast down you. You should know damn well why I keep nagging you not to be late.' Eyes popping, she pointed at the headlines in the newspaper spread over the bed.

RECESSION BITES DEEPER, CITY'S UNEMPLOYMENT HIGHEST IN THE STATE

Despairingly shaking her head, she continued, 'What with your Pa dead, ain't got no-one to turn to than you, your poor Mamma sick an all. You better not give that boss man Ackroyd any excuse to fire you,' she groaned, 'not with your color skin, unless he just died from heatstroke or heart attack.'

Willard was always in the firing line with the showroom's racist manager Rick Ackroyd; ridiculed and put down at every opportunity. Yet this vile pig of a man, unknowingly, would be instrumental in catapulting this dirt-poor youngster into another dimension. A world of unimaginable wealth, a world in which Rick Ackroyd would eagerly offer his soul to enter – even his fancy gold tooth he thought enhanced his sleazy sales smile.

Willard entered the smallest of kitchens, where one could just about swing a cat and if Willard didn't get a move on, mother and son may well have to skin one to survive! With his mother's voice following him, he shakes a packet of cereal into a bowl, adding milk, his eyes rolling in tandem with her nagging. Every day he had to cope with Sadie's lot in life. Never his own.

'If you come home early, I'll know you bin fired, in which case you better not come home at all. You hear?'

9

'Yes Mamma,' he sighed, 'I hear you Mamma.'

Her voice failing. 'And on your way out, tell my lazy sister, the one who's forgotten I live upstairs. Tell her I need her to pay me a visit more often. Once or twice a day isn't enough in this overheated prison I'm confined to. You hears, Willard?'

'Yes Mamma,' replied her son, letting out a deeper sigh. 'I hear you.'

Sadie wasn't a good patient by any means. Thankfully, Willard was a patient listener. She'd been laid up for almost two years, paralysed down one side after suffering a stroke brought on by the sudden death of her husband. Fortunately her younger sister kept an eye on her during Willard's absence. Sadie's complaint that she only checked on her once a day was an exaggeration, played out for attention.

As was always the case before leaving for work, Willard kissed his mother goodbye, but this time he sensed something wasn't right. Even with the bedroom window wide open, the air was tempered by the ever rising sun commanding the city's vibe of lethargy, yet her forehead felt cold and clammy on his lips.

'You okay, Mamma? You don't look so good. Ain't natural, so pale and your forehead cold an all.'

Sadie, impatient for her son to leave for work, slaps the newspaper on the bed. 'Take another look at that headline and stop fussing. I'm as fit as I'll ever be, Willard. Get going or that son-of-a-bitch Ackroyd will sure as hell fire you.'

Willard had no idea that his mother was heading for another stroke, far bigger than the previous one. This one would be the last. He would never get the chance to kiss her again. Living from hand to mouth might have been a different story had Willard's dreams come true. His IQ was well above average, along with his high school grades, mathematics in particular. He dreamed about being an accountant for some rich businessman or other. However, the dream he dreamed most, having a rich, baritone voice, was of being the first black Country and Western singer to be famous in Nashville. There was still a possibility, however unlikely, for one or the other to come true. Those dreams continued to thrive in his head but the reality was stark. Willard couldn't even afford the cheap bus-ride to work, having to walk the three miles to the showroom in the city's heart.

Leaving home, he headed for the impressive, glass fronted showroom of Chess Autos. Arriving, a night-duty security guard opened the gates to the high-walled yard behind the showroom. Inside, four luxury automobiles were standing there waiting for Willard to hose down, wax and polish. Being first on the premises, the yard had become Willard's private shower room. His morning ritual during the heatwave was to strip to his underpants and turn the hose on himself. A luxury that didn't cost him a cent, unless Rick Ackroyd decided to turn up earlier than his normal 9am, which was very unlikely, being a person who believed in strict rules. After cooling off, Willard was soon hosing down another macho young body, that of a powerful blood-red Thunderbird.

At 9am precisely, the stocky showroom manager marched into the yard wearing a black suit, silver tie and pristine white shirt. Dressed like an undertaker, he had just emerged from his air-conditioned limousine. The middle-aged, crew-cut, ex-marine had the complexion of a man who despised sunshine as he headed in the direction of his office across the yard at the back of the showroom. Willard, polishing the Thunderbird, raised his head as the manager passed by.

'Mornin Mr Ackroyd boss,' ventured Willard, preparing for a negative reply or being ignored altogether.

Turning abruptly, the manager huffed. 'Good morning? That depends if that Thunderbird is on the forecourt by noon, Henderson, you hear? By noon and not a minute later.' Unlocking the office door, Ackroyd entered, but not before pointing his finger at Willard threateningly. 'By noon,' he scowled.

The cleaner waved acknowledgement, smiling good-naturedly, knowing full well that Ackroyd would have wanted a disturbed look on his face. Ackroyd slammed the office door behind him in temper. Willard continued polishing the heat-seared hood.

Back in the office, cursing under his breath, the bad-tempered manager took off his jacket and loosened his tie before turning on the air-conditioning unit to the showroom. The armpits of his white shirt had turned grey with his miserable sweat, still simmering with contempt for Willard.

Always boasting to anyone who bothered to pester of his time in the marines during the Second World War, he thought he was the toughest guy on Chess Autos payroll until Willard turned up, 6ft 4, athletic and 17 stone. Ackroyd's crown would continue to wobble on his crew-cut head as long as Willard continued to literally overshadow him.

At precisely 12 noon, Ackroyd peered through a crack in the office window blind, hoping to pounce on his cleaner. But Willard's polishing had ended. The barrier arm at the entrance to the yard had already soared vertically and Willard was about to drive out and onto the showroom forecourt. Suddenly a huge crow flew over the gleaming Thunderbird and crapped on the windshield. Ackroyd, none the wiser, only aware of Willard holding a cloth and cleaning the windshield when the Thunderbird should be moving out onto the forecourt.

'Got him,' he seethed, glancing at his watch before

bouncing out of the office, making a bee-line towards the unsuspecting young employee.

Creeping up behind him, Ackroyd let rip. 'Henderson!' he yelled. Willard almost jumped out of his skin and god forbid, accidentally scores the windshield with his ring. Meanwhile, the manager almost had a seizure.

'Son of a bitch! Look what you've done!' he screamed, holding his head in his hands. Can't you do anything right? You can't even tell the time! This car should be out of here by now! Just look at this windshield. Ruined!'

Both of them perspiring heavily, Ackroyd, more so, having blown a gasket, they faced up to each other. Willard pointed his finger at the windshield and hurled his cloth to the floor in disgust. 'You scared the shit out of me, Mr Ackroyd,' he protested. 'I didn't mean it, honest, boss.'

'You didn't mean it? Scared the shit out of you? Listen, boy. I'll scare the shit out of you. You're fired!'

Willard's broad shoulders slumped on hearing the word 'fired!' It had been said so many times by his mother, almost every morning after waking. His hands, visibly trembling, held together in prayer, pleading, as did the single tear slipping down his cheek.

'No, boss,' he cried. 'I need this job real bad. My sick Mamma, she...' Ackroyd, clearly seeing the fear in his eyes stepped back a few paces, salivated venom dribbling from his mouth, spouting orders in marine-like mode. 'Get this Thunderbird back in the yard immediately,' he barked. 'Then come to the office, you're being paid off. Half day's wages!' Turning on his heels he fired a parting shot. 'But if I had my way you'd get nothing but the invoice for the damaged windshield!' With that he disappeared into his office, again slamming the door for effect.

Inside the office, wiping his brow with a handkerchief, Rick Ackroyd then turned his attention to another window in the room. This one layed bare the goings on in the showroom. Tentatively, he checked for any movement there, besides a lone salesman idling, looking bored but no doubt appreciating the air-conditioning. The huge showroom was a sea of stunning limousines, mostly Cadillacs, pristine and mirror-like, thanks to Willard's dedicated polishing. What with the sun shining through the glass-fronted showroom, every limousine sparkled like a shop full of jewels.

The manager checked his watch, clearly showing signs of nervousness. He was expecting a very important customer to show his face at any given moment and he wasn't going to be disappointed. Suddenly one of the most recognisable faces on the planet entered the showroom, like a scene from a three-dimensional movie set with no director, film crew or cameras present.

Elvis Presley, accompanied by a member of The Memphis Mafia, his loyal close friends, knew exactly where to head. The showroom's jewel in the crown, a voluptuous, voluminous pink Cadillac, waiting for him to collect and provide a good home, like a pedigree in a dog rescue centre.

Ackroyd quickly slung on his jacket and straightened his tie before checking his appearance in the office mirror. The fan in the ceiling did nothing to reduce his body temperature. His blood pressure had also risen dramatically and the half finished glass of Jack Daniel's whiskey on the office desk didn't help matters. With one intensified gulp he emptied what was left before wiping the perspiration from his brow, opening the interior door to the showroom and making a beeline for the only visitors in the showroom.

'She's all yours, Mr Presley.' He smiled for the first time that day, revealing his gold tooth as he handed the car keys over to The King, looking cool and immaculate in a red jacket and white, open collared shirt. 'All ready to go sir. You'll find the requirement you requested we worked on will be met with your approval and to the high standard we guarantee here at Chess Autos.'

With a flourish of his hand, he invited Elvis to inspect the Fleetwood's interior. Wearing sunglasses, Elvis eased his lithe body behind the steering wheel and leaned back in the seat, his famous lip curling into a satisfied smile, knowing that his mother, Gladys, was going to have the surprise of her life in less than a month's time.

Kneeling beside the stunning vehicle, Ackroyd, his temperature cooling down thanks to the air-conditioning, told Elvis about the whereabouts of the tiny button situated at the back of the glove box. When pressed, it revealed the secret compartment that had been requested.

Adjusting his sunglasses, Elvis opened the box and searched for the button. Pressing it, the compartment opened. At that point, Elvis asked Ackroyd and his companion to take a wander around the Fleetwood and check that the bodywork was in the same mint condition as when it was brought in for the refinement.

As soon as he felt no-one was watching, Elvis reached into his jacket and produced an ornate mother-of-pearl-handled Derringer pistol, then a diamond-encrusted ring and diamond necklace. He checked his surroundings again, including the office's interior window, and placed the valuable items in the secret compartment.

Meanwhile, Willard had followed his manager's instructions and got the Thunderbird lined up with the other automobiles in the yard before going to the office to collect his measly half day wages of two dollars. He was in desperation. With no chance of securing another job because of the recession and facing his mother's wrath when he arrived back home, even though she said not to bother returning if he was fired, he instinctively set about rifling the office while Ackroyd was in the showroom. It was

15

a waste of precious time. Everything worth taking was securely locked in drawers and cabinets. The wily manager had even screwed down the office desk.

As Elvis cradled the jewellery and Derringer in his hands, standing at the side of the window, peeping through and seeing it happening, Willard stepped sideways, just as Elvis checked the window. The coast was clear and the items found their way into the secret compartment, not that Willard saw it happening. Tentatively taking another look, Elvis was already out of the Cadillac, in conversation with the two men.

For Willard, the minutes dragged, desperate to get out of the oven-like office. Even with the window and door wide open and the ceiling fan playing its part, the heat was almost unbearable. Fortunately, Ackroyd happened to glance at the office window and Willard reacted, gesturing, demanding his wages.

Muttering something to Elvis, Ackroyd excused himself, striding back to the office. Red faced, he barged in, his blood pressure obviously sky high.

'What in hell's name are you doing in here. You blind or somethin?' Don't you know who I'm dealing with out there?' he raged.

Willard, perspiring from every pore in his being, coldly replied. 'You told me to line up the Thunderbird in the yard and then come to the office to collect my money. Remember?'

Ackroyd chuckled disparagingly, his gold tooth breaking through his fixed smile. It caused the hairs on Willard's neck to stand proud. 'Remember?' he mocked. 'Why should I remember anything I've ever said to you, boy? Now, take a walk. I'm busy.'

The seething manager had one more insult to spew, goading Willard to dare lay a finger on him.

'Go back to your sick momma, black boy. Tell her Rick Ackroyd fired you. Yeah?'

Without warning, a massive hand grabbed the manager's balls and yanked hard, causing him to squeal like a pig entering a slaughterhouse. Willard's passiveness was at its end. Menacingly, he said. 'Give me my money you piece of shit.'

Pained in more ways than one, Ackroyd's marine persona hoped to get him out of trouble. Defiantly, he ordered, 'Now look here, Henderson, I won't tolerate this aggressive...'

Willard squeezed harder, yanked harder, twisted harder, almost lifting the squealing pig off his feet.

'Okay. Okay. I hear you...' he yelped, heels touching the ground again.

Shaking with fear, fumbling with a jangle of keys, Ackroyd unlocked a desk drawer and gives two dollars, tenderly soothing his aching groin. Pushing him to one side, Willard reached into the drawer and helped himself to the rest of the petty cash. Towering over the now cowering ex-marine, Willard warned him.

'Now, listen here, Mr Ackroyd, boss. Next time you employ a black boy, you better show some respect, yeah? Between you and me and nobody else, I'm takin' these here extra wages on account of your generosity, okay? I don't wanna have to return and nail your two balls to the desk. Get my meaning?'

Ackroyd was lost for words. He knew he was beat. Shocked that the young buck had turned on him, he nodded that he understood. Still clutching his groin, he slumped into his office chair, his complexion back to its usual pallid self. Finding it hard to breath in the heat, he gasped, 'You'll pay for this, Henderson. I know where you live.'

Ackroyd spat at the floor contemptuously as Willard

headed out the door. Without turning, he called out, 'Don't forget, boss. Elvis is still in the building!'

Hurrying from the showroom, making his way back home, Willard prayed that by threatening to nail his scrotum to the desk, he had scared the manager enough to let him off the hook. He had no choice but to trust that his balls meant more to him than reporting a petty thief. In retrospect, he deeply regretted stealing the petty cash, around 200 dollars. If anyone was going to get nailed, it was himself. After all, Ackroyd said he knew where he lived, but he may have been bluffing hot air.

With the showroom a mile or so behind him, Willard cast a lonely figure treading the outskirts of the city. The almost deserted, dusty road ahead, simmering in the heat, gave the illusion that its surface was a pool of water. A mirage.

The roar of a speeding vehicle coming up behind him made his heart sink. Had Ackroyd put the law on his tail? 'Shit.' he mouthed, instinctively increasing his pace, for all the good it would do. The pink Cadillac flashed past him, skidded to a standstill creating a mini dust storm. Willard groaned, not thinking straight, believing it could only be Ackroyd behind the wheel. Unlikely, but remotely feasible if circumstances warranted it.

Willard need not have worried. Ackroyd was in his office, feet up on the desk, smoking a cigar and routinely refilling his glass from a bottle of Jack Daniels. Even though his nuts were still aching, he was in a good mood. Elvis had made a cash payment for the work on the Fleetwood and given a generous tip. His adversary had been fired, why make a stink about the petty cash. Chess Autos need not know about it going missing. After all, he'd done the same himself many times, and cooking the books was far more convenient than chasing Willard and having to attend the law courts.

Elvis stuck his head out the driver's window, gesturing for Willard to hop in. His eye had caught CHESS AUTOS emblazoned on the back of his work shirt. Feeling sorry for the guy having to trudge in such heat and being pleased with the work done on the Cadillac, it was the least he could do.

Willard heaved his seventeen stone frame onto the rear seat and the suspension got tested. He could hardly believe his luck. Not only had the most famous rock star in the world stopped to give him a lift, he'd be home in a few minutes with plenty of places to hide should Ackroyd have decided to turn him in.

Elvis was sure living up to his wild image, he thought, settling in for the ride. Elvis's friend and bodyguard Red West, so named because of his ginger hair, turned in his front passenger seat.

'Hey,' he said, 'ain't you the guy I saw back there in the showroom's office? You and the manager seemed to be dancing with each other, or somethin'.'

'Yeah,' replied Willard, gazing through the window. 'But we sure weren't dancing, sir.'

'Maybe just holding hands, eh?' sniffed Red, winking at Elvis.

'Nope,' said Willard cautiously, feeling uneasy about the suggestiveness inferred in the question. 'The only thing I was holding onto sir, was waiting for Mr Ackroyd to hand over my wages he owed me.'

'Ah, yes,' chuckled Red. 'Dammit, Elvis, they weren't dancing, just arguing over money.'

'There you go,' drawled Elvis, about to drive off.

'I know one thing,' frowned Red, 'that ol' manager, he got some kinda complaint down below, kept rubbin' his crotch. Right up until he waved us goodbye.'

'Say, Elvis,' whooped Red. 'Maybe that gold-toothed manager got more than a little excited about being in your company. Yeah?'

Elvis revved the powerful engine. 'Yeah,' he smiled. 'I'm told I have the same effect on a lot of girls, too. Okay, hold on. Let's see what this lady can do for me.'

Elvis hit the throttle real hard, devouring the road before them. Over the scream of the engine, Willard leaned forward, head between the two men. 'I know one thing,' he hollered. 'My boss sure has a small dick!'

Red fired back. 'How come you know, boy. You got tendencies in that department?'

Before Willard could make a point of denial, the engine suddenly lost power, gliding to a stop.

Elvis slammed the steering wheel hard with his hand. 'Oh, man,' he wailed. 'The throttle cable's snapped! don't believe it, man. We just left the showroom!'

Spitting feathers, the singer turned in his seat and finger-pointed. Willard was open mouthed in disbelief. He wasn't bothered about Elvis losing his rag and taking it out on him and being the patsy on behalf of Chess Autos. He was almost home, dry and hiding, but here he was, motionless, on a dusty deserted road. He glanced behind. There was a truck coming up, slow and easy, that was all.

'Hey boy,' scolded Elvis. 'Don't turn your back on me. What's your name?'

Willard quickly responded, sitting poker-straight, attentive. 'Henderson, sir,' he spluttered. 'Willard Henderson. I just been fired by my boss, back at the showroom, reckon he don't like my skin color, him being a racist an' all.'

Red West chipped in. 'I didn't like the color of his own skin, bein' truthful. Dead-lookin'. Grey, like the color of his hair.'

Elvis was in no mood for small talk. 'Do you know anything about car engines? We need to get rollin.'

Shrugging his shoulders, Willard explained, 'I ain't no

mechanic, Mr Presley. I was employed just to work in the backyard, making them automobiles shine like the sun before they hit the showroom for selling.'

'Holy shit,' sighed Elvis despairingly, wondering what to do next. He adjusted his aviator sunglasses. 'Okay, Red, you and me, let's high-tail it outta here, start walking, hail a cab when one comes along. As for you Willard, well, I'm makin' you responsible for takin' care of this here Cadillac, you hear? We'll call the showroom and get someone out to fix her. Ackroyd won't have a dick to scratch when I'm finished with him.'

Willard had so much to think about. If he could have wound the clock back and not lost his temper with Rick Ackroyd and not pilfered more than his entitled wages he'd be home by now, hoping his mother would understand why it wasn't his fault for getting fired. The bloody crow had a lot to answer for by crapping on the windshield. But Sadie, stroke-stricken, propped up in her bed, was now dead to the world. Her son, without realising, was now far more alone with his troubles than he could have ever imagined. By the time Elvis reached home, Willard had gathered his desperate thoughts together and made a decision. If he could reunite the snapped cable by twisting the ends together, he could rev the engine and get as far away from Memphis as possible. His mother's sister, who checked on Sadie every day, would see to her needs. He would write a letter to her as soon as he found himself in a position to do so from wherever the Fleetwood took him, explaining everything, telling his mother he loved her and would return when he thought it safe to do so, whenever that might be.

Now, crouched behind the steering wheel after successfully fixing the cable, the pink Cadillac was eating up the miles at breakneck speed. Willard Henderson, fugitive, driving with a full tank of gas, 200 dollars in his pocket and having a high IQ to his advantage, had stolen an automobile belonging to Elvis Presley. He was in deeper trouble than ever as he headed for the mighty city of New York and the anonymity, salvation and hope it may provide...

Elvis was beside himself, having made the mistake of trusting the car cleaner, cursing himself for not letting Red look after the Cadillac instead. Now he was banging his head against another brick wall, facing another dilemma caused by the theft. The blue Cadillac he had purchased and resprayed a vivid pink was to be a present for his mother Gladys, lovingly bound in a massive satin bow, along with the contents of the secret compartment: the gun and jewellery. But now it was a safe bet that the stunning automobile was either hidden in some barn or far away over the state line.

He was determined to see the look on his mother's face and his own joy as she opened her eyes to the gorgeous gift. Fortunately, time was on his side. He could get hold of another Fleetwood and respray it pink. He vowed her surprise would not be denied. With this in mind, Elvis chose not to report the Cadillac stolen, aware that once it got out that it belonged to him, Gladys would soon get to know about it. Elvis quickly ushered in his loyal old schoolfriend, Red West, to get things organised in three weeks. Red swore on his life, knowing Elvis would probably kill him if he let on to anyone about the disappearing present.

TWO

IF I CAN DREAM

66 years later: January, 2022 and the dawn of a New Year in the United Kingdom. The season's celebrations have come to an end. The hangovers of hangovers have dissipated into thin air. The country's millions wake up to the fact that Christmas has made its annual cavernous dent in almost empty bank accounts; and that that January is set to be the coldest, wettest month in years. A shotgun wedding being held in west London is in full swing in the community hall. A disco is going full blast and the bride, eight months pregnant, has managed to get up and dance on a table. Meanwhile the bridegroom's drunken, lewd behaviour is angering the bride's father to such an extent that the aforementioned shotgun wedding might well end in tragedy before the night is through!

A silver Ford Transit van, parked at the rear of the hall near the fire escape door, a fraction open, revealing a section of a stage inside, is rocking on its springs, a downpour of winter rain is pummelling its roof, drowning out the squeals, groans and other sounds of ecstasy being manufactured inside, maybe an addition to the human race. Meanwhile, a well worn mattress is taking a pummelling for the umpteenth time.

Pacer Burton, a 24-year-old Elvis Presley tribute act, is vocally expressing himself as is the 18-year-old bridesmaid, her dress, layers of cream satin, up around her waist.

Headlights from a moving car pan the van's interior, but the pair are oblivious. Suddenly, the singer notices that the disco music has stopped: the cue that he must do the same.

'Shit!' he exclaimed! 'Should be on stage, the music's stopped!'

Leaping from the back of the van, tucking in his shirt, leaving the dishevelled bridesmaid sitting up and still breathing hard, he rushed into the dressing-room behind the stage, and reappears wearing a white, rhinestone jump-suit with an acoustic guitar slung over his shoulder.

More than a third of the stage was reserved for the DJ and his musical equipment, turntables, lights and speakers. Pacer, looking like the real deal, tall, lean, hair perfectly styled even to the quiff almost touching his forehead. Reaching the edge of the cramped stage where he had set up his own sound system, he was welcomed by whoops of admiration from a gaggle of inebriated women standing in a circle in the middle of the hall, drinks in hands, clearly impressed with the lip curling tribute act smiling down at them. There were about 70 guests milling around, many of them crowding the bar, waiting to be served. Pacer slightly adjusted his microphone on its stand.

'Hi, there.' he drawled, applying his hero's stance and accent, 'It sure looks like you all having a swell time out there. Honey, you sure look beautiful standing there in your wedding dress. My, the groom sure is a lucky son of a gun let me tell you.'

Pressing a foot pedal for the backing tracks, Elvis's 'Guitar Man' blasts from the speakers and the hall comes alive when Pacer starts singing. Predictably, rock and roll jiving gymnasts commanded most of the floor, showing off their dance moves, drunkenly barging into other dancers, incoherent, with every song that Pacer entertained.

The bride's father was not the happy man he should have

been. Seated at a table laden with drink, he had already warned his new son-in-law about his unruly behaviour, bad language and blatant flirting with a pretty bridesmaid whose satin dress happened to be creased and soiled in places. She only had eyes for the handsome guy up on the stage.

What the bride must have seen in new husband, Lord knows. The only feasible explanation was the large swelling on her midriff. He was a lout, to say the least, making a fool of himself, swigging from a beer bottle, staggering towards the stage, pushing a guest out of the way as he reached it.

The bride's father, sitting alone at his table, stern-faced, looked like he was on the verge of getting to his feet and knocking the shit out of the interfering sod. Eyes rolling, he stayed where he was.

Pacer was used to dealing with these kind of morons, like it was them who decided what the rest of the crowd wanted to hear. It became a duel, Pacer singing, and a drunken slob shouting obscenities up at him overcome by the thumping loudspeakers.

Almost everyone in the hall had now joined the bride's father, focused on the inevitable. Pacer, cutting the song dead in its tracks, left the hall devoid of sound other than continuing obscenities spewing from a salivating mouth. The singer folded his arms, standing there, waiting for what he expected to hear next, based on a theme he had heard many times before.

'Hey, Elvis. Play some decent fucking music, will you? Guns and Roses or AC/DC, not this crap you keep singing! Who booked you? want a word wiv im!' Swaying, he turned around, his new audience glaring at the interfering jerk searching the room. 'Where are you?' he slurred.

Pacer leaned forward, towering over him. 'I'll tell you who booked me my friend,' he said, sarcastically. 'The father of your new wife who is crying with embarrassment, being comforted by her bridesmaids, you dick head. Go, stand by that wall over there, by the exit. That's well plastered too!'

That did it! The slob made a grab at Pacers leg, missing by a mile. Undeterred, he tried to climb onto the stage but was grabbed by his angry father-in-law and hurled to the ground, brawling before being separated. Suddenly, there was a free-for-all, with the bride and groom's families siding with each other, something not uncommon at weddings.

The village hall, now the scene of seemingly unstoppable fist-to-fist combats. Tables and chairs strewn across the dance floor, head-butting, hair-pulling, granny bashing, nail- scratching, screaming women kicking out at anything that moved, their husbands and boyfriends trying their best to stop them committing carnage. They, themselves, throwing punches at male adversaries at the same time.

Pacer, safe on the stage, was quickly packing up his musical equipment, having already taken his precious guitar back-stage to the dressing room. With one eye on the battle, the other concentrated on packing, he had noticed one of the bridesmaids standing on a chair backed against the wall to his right, looking scared to death, frantically waving for Pacer's attention.

He instantly recognised the girl he had made love to in the van. Leaping from the stage, he ushered her up, back onto it and into the dressing room, locking the door. he had some unfinished business to attend to...

The following morning, the randy singer, curled up in bed, fast asleep, his head buried under the duvet. He had performed five shows in a row and a finale he managed to squeeze in before going home. He lived with his mother, Zena, in a modest two-bedroom flat in Hammersmith, west London. There had been a time, before his father had hit the bottle and deserted them, they had lived in a nice detached house, right up until Pacer was ten-years-old when his dad lost his well-paid job. Dispirited and becoming more depressed when his mother suddenly died, he began drinking heavily, neglecting his duty to his family, spending most of his days either in bed or in the nearest pub while Zena worked in a supermarket. One night, he was involved in a fight outside a pub. Three men set upon him, leaving him unconscious. A heavily-built man, it had taken the landlord and two medics to lift him onto a stretcher. Waking up in A&E, disorientated and still drunk, he staggered out of hospital but never made his way back home. The only contact he ever made from that day on was a month later, making a phone call from a cheap bed and breakfast, a grubby hotel near Brighton on the south coast, asking Zena to send him his passport, a photo of Pacer and anything else related to his identity. At first she told him to get stuffed, but then relented, aware her husband was a complete wreck, maybe suicidal, something she couldn't bear, knowing he was a sick man who hopefully would come to his senses one day. He gave her the address of the hotel and his request was granted.

Because of the separation, flame-haired Zena, from whom Pacer inherited his good looks, was forced to foresake their house, unable to keep up with the mortgage payments, taking on the flat in Hammersmith. Pacer also took his father's valuable record collection of original vinyl albums and 45rpm singles of Elvis and the Gibson acoustic guitar that he treasured, hoping that one day he'd give them back.

It was Saturday morning and Pacer was entitled to have a lay-in. Besides gigging, he had a part-time job helping out in a garage close by. He'd gained experience working on his van and a pumped up rally car, fine-tuning the engine, making ready for race meetings, eager for the challenge of speed and thrills.

It was 1pm and the enticing smell of bacon being fried teased him into consciousness. He lay there thinking about last night. A night that would stay fresh in his mind for some time to come. Scoring twice with the bridesmaid made him sigh contentedly. Rescuing her from the war zone, into his dressing room was a good move. Afterwards, when peace had returned to the hall and he was loading the equipment into the van, he had overheard someone saying that the groom had been taken to hospital, having suffered a broken nose, fractured eye socket and painful awareness of his condition which seemed to sober him up. The barrel-chested, beer-barrelled loudmouth's surname happened to be Fuller. One could imagine the bride and groom's wedding photos, the fat slob standing next to his massively pregnant wife squeezed together beneath a stone archway leading into the church. The wedding photographer believing that by framing the couple in its doorway it would make a wonderful setting for a picture. He suggested they turned, facing each other, after seeing how uncomfortable they looked, wedged in the doorway, pertinently suggesting Mister and Misses, er… Fuller, each take a deep breath, holding it in until the camera clicked.

Still considering the previous night's shenanigans, Pacer's thoughts were abruptly interrupted.

'Pacer! Get out of bed, pronto! Breakfast!' his mother yelled from the kitchen. 'On the table in two minutes! Oh, there's a letter waiting for you. It could be the result of your audition with that TV station. It's got Island TV on it!'

Pacer leapt from his bed, dressed and was in the kitchen well within the two-minutes. The letter was on the kitchen table, propped against a sauce bottle.

'I knew that would get you to the table, sharpish,' said Zena, looking over his shoulder as he ripped open the letter. He dropped to his chair and read the contents aloud.

Dear Pacer Burton, we take pleasure in confirming that your audition for the next series of our highly successful TV show, *Star Tribute Challenge*, has been approved. Congratulations! Please acknowledge this letter by contacting us by email or telephone shown above. Rehearsals for the show begin in three weeks time.

His mother gave the open-mouthed singer a big hug. 'Well, what do you know!' she exclaimed. 'My son is going to be on the telly!'

The TV station had landed itself a high viewing audience with the show's format. Previous talent shows like *Stars In Their Eyes* were quite straightforward compared with *Star Tribute Challenge*. A panel of four celebrity judges gave marks for the contestants' performances and also tested their knowledge about the stars they were portraying, seated on a chair under a spotlight, just like *Mastermind*. One contestant at a time is eliminated, until finally, the contestant with the highest marks is awarded a month's residency in Las Vegas and £50,000 prize money. It was little wonder that Pacer auditioned for a show with all that on the cards.

Three weeks after receiving the letter, he faced the cameras in a central London studio, relieved that the programme would be going out recorded, not live. The make-up department had done a serious job on his face, as would have been done to Elvis, even adding a touch of mascara, something Elvis insisted on, his eyes being on the small size.

Casually attired in a white, open-necked cowboy shirt, tight blue jeans and his Gibson guitar slung over his shoulders, studio lights blazing on him, he looked the business.

The presenter introduced him and Pacer steamed into Presley's first hit, 'That's Alright Mama'. The studio audience lapped it up. Afterwards, the lights dimmed and a spotlight with a bluish tinge, concentrated on his upper body.

The four judges lined in front of him, below the stage, looked impressed with his performance as they prepared to question him on his knowledge about the King of Rock and Roll.

First judge: 'Hello Pacer, you really got the audience on your side with that song. Now, if you can answer my question to match that performance, we could well be seeing you next week. Can you tell me Elvis's mother's first name?'

Pacer. 'Gladys.' (correct).

Second judge: What was Elvis's employment before he became famous?'

Pacer: 'A truck driver.' (correct).

Third judge: 'Name me the Elvis record that was released in the same year he died?'

Pacer: 'Way Down.' (correct).

Fourth judge: 'And finally, Pacer. What was the name given to Elvis's group of loyal friends?'

Pacer: 'The Memphis Mafia.' (correct). Audience applause.

Pacer had sailed through the first set of questions, going through to the next round and the following one while other unfortunate acts were being sent home, including Lady Gaga and Michael Bublé, the questions becoming harder every week. Then, after correctly answering three of the judges' questions, after knocking them out with Elvis's 'Suspicious Minds'...

The last judge: 'Okay, Pacer, you've done so well in this competition, vocally as well as your ability in answering correctly every question thrown at you throughout, on the life and times of The King, has been quite remarkable so good luck with this challenging last question. Pacer had performed 'Suspicious Minds' without playing his guitar this time, in the glare of the studio lights, wearing a black leather outfit similar to the one Elvis had worn on his comeback TV show in June, 1968, performing his hits on a small stage with only a few musicians backing him. Now, with the studio orchestra out of sight relaying the music from another studio nearby, he stood there alone, feeling naked without his guitar to hold. All he had to hold on to now was a microphone, the chair and his nerve. The questions were getting harder and harder every week and it was the semi-final. The show's title would certainly be living up to its name on this occasion.

Pacer was perspiring after putting everything he had into his performance. Had he known the question the last judge was going to hit him with, he would have been sweating buckets.

'Are you ready to go?' asked the judge, looking down at the question he was about to serve on the clearly nervous-looking singer.

'Yeah' came the reply, accompanied by a nervous cough.

'Okay. Give the venue and date of Elvis's final concert before he died, and the set list of his act.'

Pacer's eyes glazed over on hearing the question, thinking he wasn't going to get through this. The seconds ticked away, until...

'Elvis performed his final concert on June 25th, 1977, at Market Square Arena in Indianapolis, before an audience of 18,000.' Pausing, he went on. 'The set list: 'See See Rider', 'I Got A Woman' coupled with 'Amen', 'Love Me', 'Fairytale', 'You Gave Me A Mountain', 'Jailhouse Rock', 'O Sole Mio' coupled with 'It's Now Or Never'.'

Beads of perspiration were now gelling together on his forehead, a crucial sign that Pacer's backlog of recollections were beginning to affect his confidence and concentration. Nevertheless, he soldiered on. 'Then...' he faltered, 'a medley of hits: 'Little Sister', 'Teddy Bear' and 'Don't Be Cruel'. 'Release Me', 'I Can't Stop Loving You', 'Bridge

Over Troubled Water"... err ... "Early Morning Rain',
'What'd I Say', 'Johnny B. Goode" ... um ... "I Really Don't
Want To Know". A frustrated sigh, wiping beads of sweat
off his forehead, Pacer ventured. "Hurt". His eyes
questioning its validity for a moment before smiling with a
sense of relief. 'Elvis then sang 'Hound Dog' and the song
he always finished with, 'Can't Help Falling In Love'.'

Mesmerised by his ability to answer such a difficult and
challenging question, the audience applauded, fervently
expressing their solidarity. Meanwhile, Pacer looked
drained, praying he hadn't cocked things up and not
disappointed his mother, let alone the studio audience. Even
the judges had joined them in clapping along. Then came
the moment of truth.

The judge who had presented Pacer with the question
raised his hand in a salute. 'I must congratulate you, Pacer,'
he smiled, generously. 'That was a tall order to accomplish.
A mighty challenge and it showed how much research
you've done on Elvis. But again, as you've already said, he's
your hero and you are his biggest fan.'

The judge's demeanour then changed. He cleared his
throat. 'However, it has to be said that you did happen to
slip up once, and um...there is no room for mistakes at this
stage, it being the semi-final. You were perfect in naming
the venue that Elvis played before his death, and perfect in
naming all the songs in Elvis's set. But the full set also
included the music he walked on stage with. 'Also Sprach
Zarathustra' as was used in the movie, *2001. A Space
Odyssey*. The judge gave an enormous over the top sigh.
'Sorry, Pacer.'

Turning in his seat, making small-talk with the other
judges, the theme music for the programme kicked in,
cameras now concentrating on the show's presenter
reminding viewers to tune in next week, not to miss the final.

Meanwhile, Pacer's mother had already left her seat in the audience, hurrying across the studio floor, towards the podium where her son remained, sad-faced, microphone hanging limp in his hand. Troubled tears running down her cheeks, Zena hugged the dejected, rejected singer, until the studio lights dimmed, indicating that it was time to leave.

Yes, it was true, the classical instrumental piece was technically part of the set but unfair on the lad. It was a trick question that would have stumped the King of Rock and Roll himself!

Deep in the Buckinghamshire countryside, 30 miles north of London, in a darkened, wood-panelled room illuminated by a large slim-line television, the credits were rolling at the end of Star Tribute Challenge, the week in which Pacer's dream of winning had gone up in smoke. Suddenly the room was plunged into blackness and silence, courtesy of the TV remote control being activated. But for the rustling of a duvet on a king-size bed, one would have not known it was occupied. Then a voice broke the room's quietude. 'That boy deserved to win. It was a set up. I liked him.'

A lot of viewers liked Pacer Burton, much of it to do with the show's popular video footage about the contestants' lives in general. It showed him working on car engines, his love of rally driving and the life and times of his hero, Elvis. It showed the superstar's photos on his bedroom wall and the valuable collection of Presley albums stashed under his bed. It was little wonder he knew the set-list question off by heart. The show's producer and his absorbed interest in the winning act may have had something to do with 'Also Sprach Zarathustra'.

Three

RAGS TO RICHES

Something good usually comes from something bad, it being the balance of nature. The fact that Pacer had lost out on the show under circumstances that looked dodgy, probably instigated by the infatuated producer, had made the singer a talking point, with many viewers writing in, complaining about the raw deal he had been dealt, triggering a couple of national newspapers to print their readers' concerns, one of them stirring things up by asking them to take a vote on it. This positive publicity for Pacer was invaluable, equivalent to paying a load of cash for a decent advert in the newspaper. The singer's booking agent became inundated with venues wanting the talented performer to appear in them. Good certainly came knocking on the singer's door with one particular booking, making Star Tribute Challenge seem like a nonsense compared to a far more dangerous one waiting for him in the not too distant future.

Winter was on the wane and April making its mark, its menu of restless change of temperatures resulting in heavy showers, blustery winds and cold snaps. It was around 7.00pm when Pacer's van pulled up outside The Dockers Tavern, an eighteenth-century pub in East London, in the heart of the Isle of Dogs. Its postal address, Canary Wharf, one of the main financial centres in the world, containing many high-rise skyscrapers. The Dockers Tavern, a Grade

Two listed building squeezed in, overshadowed by younger trespassers boldly commanding acre upon acre of real estate.

Standing beside his van, Pacer gazed at the night sky and twinkling lights shining from pillars of high-rise offices always open for business on every time zone around the world. He marvelled at the 02 Arena, half a mile away on the other side of the winding River Thames, the domed venue resembling a flying saucer with aliens about to emerge and plunder the rich and powerful inhabitants of Canary Wharf, before moving further afield with the same intent, drawn to Hatton Gardens, London's jewellery quarter and the centre of diamond trade in the United Kingdom, using their superior mental powers of detection.

It had taken Pacer almost two hours to cover the few miles from Hammersmith to The Isle of Dogs (the name given to the area in the sixteenth century because of the number of dead dogs that washed up on its banks). As usual, the evening rush hour traffic had been a nightmare to weave through. One mayhem after another, judging by the boisterous laughter and chatter emanating from the crammed establishment serving champagne as its most popular beverage, followed by spirits and the odd pint of beer. Cider certainly wasn't on the list.

Unloading his PA system from the van, Pacer concluded that weaving his way through the crowd, where he assumed he was going to perform, would be like making his way across London.

Just as he was about to go in, he was distracted by the creaking of the tavern's sign hanging above his head, swayed by a sudden gust of wind, its fitful lighting illuminating a sailing ship, flickering wildly, as though sending a SOS.

Having set up his amp in a corner of the busy, bustling ale house, Pacer took in his surroundings. He had felt, on entering the ancient tavern, he had travelled 250 years into the past, the interior as bygone as the outside. He imagined the ghosts of Long John Silver and his Treasure Island shipmates singing sea-shanties and spilling their frothing tankards as they danced a jig to a screeching violin. The room was like an enormous sea captain's cabin, its oak-panelled walls awash with paintings of sailing ships, early steamships, portraits of long-dead masters smoking clay pipes; and other seafaring paraphernalia. The oak tables and chairs had served their purpose from the day the tavern first opened to the public. Pinpricked by voracious woodworm but exterminated before they could cause even more damage, had left their calling cards. The antique wood faded by age and overuse of polish, gave the surfaces a grey, deathly sheen in places but added to the charm of being locked in time, just like the pub. However, that wasn't the case with its clientele. Not one sea-salt customer could be seen, having been vanquished long ago by the invasion of city slickers in their fine suits and designer wear, who moved in when Canary Wharf, which took its name from the sea trade with the Canary Islands, became the world's leading financial hub. The Dockers Tavern was only one or two pubs not razed to the ground because of their heritage distinction, the others making room for the many skyscrapers that now stood there. The Dockers Tavern was now catering for more refined tastes in alcohol, men and women customers alike, spending loads of easy money acquired by pleasing shareholders, buying exotic drinks when tiring of consuming champagne from their chilled buckets lined up along the bar.

On this occasion, the booking being a one-off pub gig, Pacer hadn't brought along one of his Presley outfits, which was fortunate, there was nowhere to change.

Wearing a black tee-shirt and trousers, he looked more

like a James Bond tribute, but instead of a Walther P38, the singer was holding a Gibson guitar.

It was almost 9pm, time for him to entertain the financial brains behind American Express, Apple, Barclays, to name just a few of the major businesses that rented offices in the area. Some of the loudmouths at the bar were no more than boastful, overpaid digit-counting clerks, while cleverer colleagues seated nearby were in a different league altogether, quietly sipping expensive champagne, cognac and wine, never foolish enough to slip up about their massive salaries, some higher than their immediate superiors.

Apprehensively trying to determine what sort of reaction he would get from a load of inebriated digit-heads who didn't seem to have the slightest awareness that Elvis hadn't left the building, or ever been in it, Pacer didn't look comfortable at all.

His vexations were interrupted by a round of applause aimed at the pub's manager waltzing down the stairway at the side of the bar, fresh from her boudoir upstairs. The ex-drag queen, well into her sixties, had traded in her club-circuit act, preferring a more static lifestyle, such as propping up the bar while giving orders to her staff.

Wearing a Dolly Parton wig and a flowing pink evening gown weighed down with chunky costume jewellery, Sherry Starr threaded her way through the crowds making a beeline for Pacer. Having downed a litre of vodka that day, with not a hint that she had done so, the buxom queen pressed her dainty illegitimate nose against the back of her Chanel perfumed wrist before opening her lipstick lips.

'Well, darling', she purred. 'I can see you've managed to plug in your enormous equipment.' Sherry's voice, deep as the folds in her neck had confirmed Pacer's suspicions, that Sherry Starr had been born with a pair of balls.

'I'm Sherry Starr, landlady of this joint,' she groaned,

turning round and scanning the room. 'There's only room for one star in this here establishment,' she continued, flourishing a bangled, jewellery-jangled hand. 'Sherry Starr!'

Turning, flashing her chimney-sweep eyelashes at the dumfounded singer, believing that she was about to send him packing, the old draq queen smiled. 'But I caved in on this occasion, Elvis. Firstly, I don't have to pay your fee, according to your agent it's all been arranged, and secondly, I saw you get shafted on that TV show you were on. I was tempted to hurl my high-heels at the telly. You was robbed, my son.'

Pacer shrugged his shoulders. 'I can't argue at that,' he sighed. 'I've heard the same from a load of people. Even the national newspapers.'

Sherry gave the singer a hearty slap on his back. 'Bollocks to 'em,' she winked. 'Keep at it. One day, you may find yourself playing the O2, like that American midget, Bette Midler, she's appearing there tonight. I was singing Lee Greenwood's 'The Wind Beneath My Wings' six years before she had a bloody hit with it. For all the notice this lot took of me back then, might as well had been singing 'The Old Rugged Cross'. But when she got into the charts, that's all these obsessed, money grabbing top loaders wanted to hear. Watch this, darling.'

Sherry seated herself at the upright piano close by, against the wall. With a flourish of the keys, she dived straight into 'The Wind Beneath My Wings', her voice, deeper than Barry White's, bellowing like a ship's foghorn. Finishing the classic number, curtseying to her applauding customers, she opened a window and yelled, 'Hear that, Midler?! That was the original Greenwood version, the best! Up yours!'

Cheering also went up from her customers as she closed the window and stood in front of the bemused singer, wondering what she was going to get up to next. After all, she had told him there was only one star in the room.

Sherry Starr.

With one hand holding the microphone stand, the other adjusting the mic, she blew into it, checking that it was working. 'Okay, settle down, settle down you high rollers. For one night only and at great expense, I demand that you all give this handsome young man the applause he deserves, especially those of you who saw him perform on the telly, that crap show, Star Tribute Challenge. I call it crap because this kid was set up to lose, predetermined and bloody fixed if you ask me.'

The old trouper, still pumped up with adrenaline after her energetic offering, paused to catch her breath and wipe her brow. 'So now, put your moneyed hands together for the one and only, the best Elvis tribute you'll ever get to see. Pacer Burton as the King of Rock and Roll!'

Turning, Sherry whispered in his ear. 'Give it all you got, kid, or you may find this lot tossing £20 notes at you, telling you to stop singing.'

On hearing that, Pacer thought it wouldn't be a bad compromise in the scheme of things, being paid off by the punters and still receive his gig money. Pressing his footswitch, the intro to 'Don't Be Cruel' blasted from the speakers.

Forty-five minutes later, a relieved Pacer Burton was bowing, not picking up notes off the floor but to an appreciative audience giving him some sound applause for a highly professional performance. Sherry grabbed the mic from its stand, holding it with one hand and clapping against it with the other, amplifying the claps. She had been standing at the bar during the act, knocking back the vodka and after being at it most of the day, she was feeling the effects.

Losing her grip on the mic, it crashed to the floor, slid across, ending at the feet of an old man in a wheelchair. Squeezed behind him, along with the fraternity who had gathered to be closer to the entertainer, a suave Mediterranean-looking man, about forty, smart-suited, handsome enough to melt any fair maiden's heart, had a protective stance about him, giving a hint of being the chairbound's carer. Swaddled in an expensive cashmere blanket he had adventurously leaned forward and picked up the microphone with his bony fingers before Pacer, Sherry, his carer or anyone else in the room could have stopped him.

Watery eyed, his face etched with chronic pain, the sick, shadow of the man he once was, handed over the microphone to its owner, standing next to him.

'Oh, thanks,' winced Pacer. 'You shouldn't have gone to such trouble, you know.'

'That was some show you put on,' came the frail reply almost indiscernible in the packed pub. 'You're good, real good. By the way, I think you should know that I'm your paymaster, son,' he wheezed. 'It was me that got you in this here place, and I'll be damned if I ain't looking for you to perform another gig for me. Now then, go sing an encore. Otherwise these here folk will be on your tail. And when you're done, we need to talk. Somewhere private I got in mind.'

Ten minutes later Pacer found himself in the sumptuous rear seat of a silver Rolls Royce Phantom parked outside the pub. Beside him, coughing spasmodically into a red silk handkerchief, the phlegm of a dying man. In the driver's seat, his concerned Italian chauffeur, keeping an eye on his own paymaster.

Regaining his composure the older man slowly turned and faced the much younger man. Pacer was unsure why he agreed to find himself in such an unsettling, unpredictable setting, sitting next to a complete stranger who looked as though he was about to keel over before passing over!

The seconds ticked away. Then, in measured tones, 'Tell me, how would you like to earn a million pounds, your fee for the gig of your lifetime?' His eyes narrowed, waiting for Pacer's reply. Would it be a positive one, or would the kid burst out laughing? He did neither.

'Well,' he said, blandly, 'only if it's around the corner, know what I mean? Not too far, like.'

'I like your sense of humour, boy,' he smiled. It must have tickled his throat as well, coughing, 'because you're sure gonna need it if you take on this job I'm offering you.'

Pacer's mind was racing by now. He could see that the old man was seriously ill but what about his head? Million pounds for the gig of a lifetime? He glanced at the chauffeur, hoping he might clarify his boss's mystifying dialogue. But the driver was looking straight ahead through the windscreen, seemingly uninterested.

Pacer's hand was on the Rolls's door handle. The weird situation was beginning to freak him out, he was on the verge of making a quick exit back into the pub but decided to keep the humour going for a while, along with some kind of composure.

'A million pounds, you say. What do you want me to do, steal the Crown Jewels? That would take a sense of humour, I reckon. Besides, I don't even know who you are; your name, for instance.'

'My name?' The man sighed, as though he didn't seem to think it of any significance. 'Henderson. Willard Henderson.' Bowing his head, he muttered, 'and as far as the Crown Jewels are concerned, my stealin' days are long gone behind me. A young man's desperation, boy.'

He fell silent, reliving events from his past. Seeing how emotional he was becoming, Pacer broke the uneasy atmosphere. 'This gig you're talking about, Mr Henderson,' he asked. 'I hope it's about music, not some dodgy caper you're setting up. If so, count me out. I'm not interested.'

Henderson looked mildly surprised. 'I've already told you all you need to know about my criminal past, it belonged to my misspent youth. This challenge I'm asking you to take on, even though you failed, unfairly, regarding your recent television appearance, I feel confident enough to believe you won't fail this one. Yes, it is connected with music, the kind you're used to playing, rock and roll.' Pausing, he wiped away the saliva building up in the corners of his mouth, using the handkerchief permanently held in his permanently trembling hand. Frustration presented itself in his voice, deep as a well. 'Son, I have to tell you before I go any further, my days are numbered. There isn't much time left for me to put my house in order. What I want you to do for me, it's all above board, I promise you. Look, here's my business card. Tell me you'll call me in two day's time. You won't regret it.'

Pacer watched the silver Rolls glide away from the pub, heading in the direction of the maze of skyscrapers where Henderson owned a luxurious apartment. Before his incurable cancer worsened, Henderson directed his lucrative stockmarket and other business interests from it, being right in the heart of the financial district.

Standing beneath the pub's sign, flickering in a light breeze, Pacer produced one of Henderson's cards. It read: Willard Henderson. Crighton Manor, Chesham, Bucks. BU14 6SL. Tel: 01862 226200.

Having taken his prescribed medication, along with a couple of powerful sleeping pills, Willard Henderson retired to his king-sized four-poster bed in Cabot Square, long before Pacer would arrive home. Driving there, across London, aware that the old fella hadn't revealed anything about what he had in mind, other than a vague comment about the era of rock and roll, the singer toyed with the idea that having paid for his gig, Henderson must be an ardent admirer of Elvis, visiting the pub to see him performing live. Maybe he wanted him to sing at his impending funeral. But a million pounds? No way, thought Pacer, he could have hired the Pope for that amount, giving him his personal blessing. One of Henderson's sleeping pills would have been a blessing too, for someone heading for Hammersmith that night.

Two Days Later. Crighton Manor

Willard Henderson was now a multimillionaire, via the well-worn passage that leads from rags to riches. Meanwhile his glamorous private nurse, Tanya Brooks, had the kind of legs that Sherry Starr would have cut off her own for, along with a figure to match. The Manor's landscape gardener, supposedly trimming his maze, almost fell off his ladder when she leaned in and helped her boss out of the Rolls while his chauffeur, Dino Rosetti, stood by with his wheelchair and a blanket to wrap around his frail body.

The Manor's forecourt could have held four Rolls Royces with room to spare, as the trio entered the eighteenth-century red-bricked fortress-like citadel with its turrets and high-stacked chimneys topped with dozens of pots. The vast building was a breath-taking sight for any visitor, other than some earl or duke, along with Richard Branson perhaps. Greek pillars, two on each side, flanked a massive studded oak door through which they entered.

Coincidentally, as the nurse closed the door behind her and the chauffeur wheeled his charge across the cathedral-like hallway into the library, the hallway phone rang and Tanya Brooks answered it, her voice, sultry and seductive as a humid sauna. 'Hello, the Henderson residence,' her pouting lips touching the end of the house phone.

'Oh, hello, Mr Henderson asked me to call him today. My name is Pacer Burton, the Elvis tribute singer. He came along to watch my act a couple of days ago.'

The brunette stroked her shoulder-length hair, frowning. 'I'm sorry. Mr Henderson's not been in any position to attend such an event. I don't know how you've obtained this number, but this isn't the same Mr Henderson you're enquiring about. I'm sure he wouldn't be seen attending an Elvis tribute...'

Dino Rosetti, having made his boss feel comfortable at his desk in the library, had returned to the hallway, overheard the nurse mentioning Elvis and had quickly taken the phone off her, just as she was about to hang up.

'Ello, si,' he said, 'I Mr Henderson's driver. You Pacer Burton, yes? We meet at pub. Mr Henderson hoping you call him. Possible you come to Crighton Manor tonight?'

Pacer, from his smart phone, working on an engine at the garage, replied, 'Yes, no problem, I'll punch in your post code on my sat-nav. 7pm you say?'

'Si. I tell Mr Henderson you come?'

'Definitely,' said Pacer, ending the call, dropping tools and getting out of his overalls.

Later that day, he was on his way to the Manor, 30 miles north-west of the Hammersmith flat, wisely driving the Transit, believing it not a good idea to arrive in his rally car, sporting half-a-dozen headlights hanging from a bar, its cabin stripped to a skeletal cage.

The sat-nav indicated that the Transit should leave the A41, turn left along the A476, and after a mile, go down a narrow country lane, through a vast forest that seemed to go on forever. Suddenly, to Pacer's dismay, the sat-nav lost its signal. The forest darkened as the sun continued to set.

'Shit,' he exclaimed, having visions of Henderson turning him away if he was late arriving. That is, if he ever managed to find the place.

He grabbed his mobile and rang the Manor, but the signal it gave was...no signal. Pacer had two choices. Turn around, out of the forest blocking the mobile's signal. Or carry on and pray he didn't come across any crossroads, giving him even more trouble. It was nearing 7pm. Pacer was about to turn on his headlights when, to his relief, he left the forest behind. The lane continued for another quarter of a mile, coming to a dead end. Before him, a high stone wall with ornate, wrought-iron gates supported by white pillars. Atop of each pillar, the bronze sculpture of a fearsome-looking Doberman, perhaps an indication of what could be expected on the other side.

Pacer drove up to the gates, got out and pressed the intercom button on one of the pillars. Waiting there, like a butcher delivering dog meat, the CCTV camera above him showed that the singer had arrived. As the gates slowly opened, a voice from the intercom instructed him to drive up to the Manor.

The sight before him, at the end of the long driveway bordered by bushes, flowerbeds, and lawns that seemed to go on forever, made his eyes dazzle, not only by such splendour but also the fiery sunset, low behind the magnificent Manor, giving the impression that the building was ablaze. Pacer was in nervous thrall of it all as he drew into the forecourt. Three figures were in the open doorway, silhouetted by the glow of chandeliers hanging from the ceiling in the vast hallway. One was in an automatic wheelchair. Dino Rosetti was stood on his right; Tanya Brooks in her nurse's uniform on her patient's left, with a blanket folded on her arm, should it be required by the Lord of the Manor.

Pacer alighted from the Transit, into the chilliness of dusk. What left him cold was the hairy shape of a large dog bearing down on him from what seemed out of nowhere, leaping up at him, barking like crazy. The startled visitor was about to scramble back into the van when he heard the chauffeur shouting, 'Don't worry! He greet you! He lika you!'

Was Pacer glad to hear those words.

After seeing those Dobermans on their pedestals, he thought he was going to be torn to pieces by the real thing lurking inside. However, the animal sniffing at his shoes and furiously wagging its tail looked nothing like a fearsome Doberman Pincher, just a harmless, cuddly Golden Retriever.

Once akin to a giant oak tree but now resembling a diseased elm, Willard Henderson leaned forward in his wheelchair, his hand ready and perhaps eager to clasp Pacer's.

'Welcome to Crighton Manor, kid,' he smiled. 'If I could have gotten out of this here damn thing, I think I might have given you a hug instead of my hand, coming all this way to see an old man, after not telling you what it's all about. You made the right decision, boy,' he wheezed. 'Yeah, the right decision.'

He looked up at the nurse, raising his thin-fleshed hand. 'Tanya,' he sighed, 'take me inside. I wanna introduce this young man to a girlfriend of mine.' Nodding to Pacer, 'I reckon you and she are gonna get along real fine, son. Just you see.'

The foursome and Rex the Labrador made their way into the hallway. Before closing the studded oak door behind them, Rosetti's gaze lingered beyond the forest, the distant shimmering lights of Hemel Hempstead twinkling like acres of glowworms feasting on evening dewdrop slugs and snails. The loyal chauffeur wondered where his own next meal-ticket would come from, after his boss had died. The squared-jawed Italian had worked for Henderson for twenty years, after he became a widower. Skiing in the Italian Alps, his English wife, son, along with his driver, perished in an avalanche. Their ski instructor, Dino Rosetti, managed to rescue Willard, eventually becoming his chauffeur and confidant.

The extensive hallway had all the features one would have expected from an eighteenth-century Manor. The grand staircase, antique furnishings, walls almost concealed by painting by notable artists, some captured in heavy, gilded frames, a struggle for anyone to carry, such as the groundsman/handyman living in the gatehouse with his wife, also employed by Henderson, the Manor's housekeeper.

Following Henderson in his powered wheelchair gliding across the hallway in the direction of the library, accompanied by his nurse, Pacer was blown away by his surroundings, like the impressive suit of armour on guard outside the library.

Relieving Tanya of her duties for the rest of the evening, Henderson invited Pacer to follow him into the library. Distracted, his eyes focused on the nurse's hip-swerving posterior, the hot-trot singer accidentally bumped into the wheelchair.

'Okay, I forgive you,' said Henderson, chuckling to himself. 'I feel your pain. I was young once.'

Pacer immediately apologised but it was brushed aside with a wearied flourish. 'Quiet, we're in a library now,' he sighed. 'Not that there's anyone here complaining, except maybe a ghost or two.'

Again, Pacer was taken aback. The oak-panelled room with its high ceiling must have contained thousands of books of every description on every subject one could imagine, fact or fiction.

Turning round in the chair facing the singer, Henderson said, 'Pacer, you should have won that damn TV show you were on. I was impressed with you from day one and I got to know a lot about you. That sob story about your father leaving home and not coming back. I know it's sad, but it happens, kid.'

'They made me tell that story about my father,' came the defensive reply. 'All those contestants were asked to do the same. I wasn't keen on the idea but they insisted.'

Henderson didn't seem aware that he had struck a nerve. 'The thing is, son, what with you being so wrapped up with Elvis, knowing so much about him and how keen you sounded when talking 'bout cars, knowing how to handle 'em and working on their engines an' all, you fitted the bill for what I'm about to introduce you to.'

Asking for Pacer's hand, he slowly rose from the wheelchair, supporting himself with his ornate, gold-handled cane. Back in the day, when Willard had lifted Rick Ackroyd off his feet by his balls, he had stood almost a foot taller than the manager but Old Father Time and the vulgarities of cancer had reduced him to a withered shadow of his former self, too weak even to raise himself by the balls of his feet, let alone Ackroyd's testicles.

Shakily gripping Pacer's hand, he continued. 'Kid, see all this opulence around you, you'd think I was a cultured, highfalutin' aristocrat type of fella. Don't believe it. All these books you see here, that whole lot of paintings, other fancy stuff out in the hall? Much of it came with this place when I bought it, part of the deal when the owner moved out. Over the years, the stock market has been more than good to me, by far. That's why I'm in such a good position to offer you this million pounds.'

Henderson raised an eyebrow, waiting for Pacer to reply. But the library stayed silent.

'So,' he continued, 'now that we've become more acquainted, I'd like you to follow me. There ain't many folk who can get me to my feet these days. Shows how much I want your services. Shows how much I like you.'

From the library, they entered another oak-panelled room, this one smaller, sparsely furnished, dominated by a king-sized bed, huge slimline TV and diamond-latticed bay window. Close to the bed stood an oxygen cylinder and medical apparatus.

'Welcome to my departure lounge,' sighed Willard. 'This is where I hole up every night. Can't make it up that staircase, but I'm damned if I'll spoil the look of it with some cranky-looking stair lift.'

He pointed at a door in a corner of the room. 'See that door over there, it leads to a garage which I used to keep two of my limousines. I use it for a different purpose now. Let's take a look.'

Undeterred by his obvious frailty, he made his way forward, unsteadily, but with an eager sense of purpose, closely followed by his Labrador and Pacer. Taking a key from his dressing gown, he asked the singer to unlock the door. As it opened, Pacer was met by a rush of thermostatically controlled air. Suddenly, from its darkness, Elvis's Space Odyssey intro filled the air, setting off a fusion of flashing lights bathing the white-walled room with their coloured brilliance. There, presenting herself in the centre of the room, an antiquity of American splendour, a pink Fleetwood Cadillac, the one that a young, despondent, desperate black-American snatched, way back in '56.

Four

RETURN TO SENDER

Pacer stood in the doorway, rigid, as though he had been turned to stone, his unblinking eyes almost proving the point. The fanfare of music quickly ended. The only sound was the heavy breathing of a man hankering, not for the promise of eternal life but eternal sleep. Aware that he had been a thief and a vagabond, Willard didn't relish the idea of going to hell, shovelling coal into a furnace.

Sidling up to the entranced singer, 'Well, what do you think of her?' he smiled. 'Told you I wanted to introduce my girlfriend to you. Don't just stand there with your mouth wide open with nothin' coming from it.'

Only two years ago Pacer had visited Graceland and drooled over the Pink Cadillac on display there. Now he could hardly believe his eyes, the old man conceiving a perfect replica of the iconic Fleetwood, placing it on display in such a theatrical manner. Glancing at the garage walls, awash with Elvis memorabilia, he concluded that Henderson wasn't an Elvis enthusiast but an infatuated, obsessed fan!

'Amazing. Just amazing, man,' he whispered. 'Perfect. Just like the real deal.'

Henderson smiled. 'Go, take a walk around her. You won't find any imperfections. Not on this here beauty. Oh, by the way, she is the real deal, boy, every nut and bolt on her. That old Cadillac on display in Graceland is pure enough. I heard told, Elvis's mother was blown away when her son gave it to her, back in '56. But that ain't half the story.'

Leaving Pacer touring the voluminous, voluptuous automobile, her proud owner sat himself in a comfortable Regency wing-backed chair. Pacer, having done the rounds with the Cadillac, joined his rich companion, telling him how impressed he was with the car, asking why he had it on display in the middle of nowhere. Everything about her looked pristine. Tyres looked as though they hadn't touched any other surface than where she stood. Henderson enlightened him.

'Oh, she's been seen alright. Over the years I've invited members of Elvis Presley's UK fan base many times. I wouldn't have wanted to keep her to myself, she's too cute for that. I think of this place being a bit of a shrine to the King; had the garage all cleaned up after he died in 1977, collected some memorabilia about his life, his career, short that it was. All that you see here is like your own career, a tribute.'

Pacer sighed. 'I thought I was a big fan of Elvis Mr Henderson but you put me to shame. All I got is a pile of his albums.'

'Well, son, tell truth, I ain't never been a big fan of his. I was always into soul music, even sang in a band when I was younger. But I owe Elvis a huge debt. You see, if it wasn't for him I would have probably remained a dirt-poor black boy growing up in Memphis, Tennessee. All that you see around you, the Manor, the money, the makings of me, would have been just a fairytale, just a dream. Listen, kid, pull up that chair over there, sit with me. I got to tell you something you need to know...'

Willard told his visitor about the day he lost his job at Chess Autos, his hatred of his racist boss, Ackroyd, and how he came to steal the Cadillac.

'Leavin' my sick mama and running away was hard, but I was a kid without a job no more. It was a stupid, impulsive thing to do, takin' that Cadillac, I know. I figured it would help pay her medical bills, but then I heard she had died and been buried soon after I hightailed it. I holed up at my cousin's place, 30 miles outside Memphis. We sprayed it a different colour. Huh, you can understand why,' he chuckled. 'Gave her false number plates.

'Elvis got hold of another Fleetwood in time for his mama's surprise, exactly the same specifications, spraying it pink again. Elvis made sure no-one talked about what happened. Gladys didn't know any different. It would have spoilt her party.

'Anyway, after layin' low for a while with my cousin, I headed for New York, melting into the crowds where I felt safe. I had a good head on me, wheelin' and dealin'. I got lucky and got rich. Never did let that old Cadillac go, knowing about its history. I got married to an English rose, she had skin like alabaster. Came here, living in England where she bore me a son. They both died, out skiing. Buried in an avalanche 20 years ago. It broke my heart and I...'

Pacer had hung onto every word that had been said. Henderson had painted for him one hell of a story, one that was as fascinating as it was powerful. But then he revealed its tragic ending. At that point the storyteller's head hung sickle-shaped in sadness. But then, when he looked up, his deep brown eyes met with Pacer's aquatic blue. Almost ready to flow.

Composing himself, the old man asked the singer to help him from the chair, groaning. 'I've let loose more than I intended, son. Much too much. Let's get back to that library, it's where you're about to find out what I have in mind for you. That is, if you agree.'

Feeling more comfortable, being back in his wheelchair,

behind his impressive oak desk, Pacer seated on the other side, Henderson opened with, 'Do you know whose 45th anniversary is coming up, later this year?'

Pacer was taken aback and his face showed it. He thought the first words coming from Henderson's mouth would have contained a semblance of what he had in mind for him. After all, they were the last words he'd spoken in the other room. But then the question clicked.

'Forty-five years since Elvis died in 1977. It now being 2022,' answered Pacer. 'This coming August. Right?'

'Right,' said Henderson, reaching down, opening one of the desk's drawers and handing Pacer a piece of paper and retaining one for himself. 'I know that date is important to you, Pacer, being aware of almost every other important occasion that Elvis attended, especially this being his last one, but it's a very important anniversary to me, also. A date of deliverance. Read what's on that piece of paper.'

'Okay,' replied Pacer, leaning forward in his seat, reading the contents before him.

> I, Willard Henderson, being of sound mind, hereby agrees to pay the undersigned, Pacer Burton, One Million Pounds on completion of his personal delivery to the gates of Graceland, Memphis, Tennessee, the spiritual home of Elvis Presley, one pink 1956 Fleetwood Cadillac, complete with original documents relating to its purchase. The legal owner(s) of the said automobile being Elvis Presley's estate. To be delivered on or before the forty-fifth anniversary of his death.
>
> Signed
> Pacer Burton.
>
> Signed
> Willard Henderson.

Pacer didn't know what to think or what to say. The wheels

spinning in his head were turning faster than any rally car he'd ever driven. It dawned on him, at last, what Henderson had hidden up his dressing-gown sleeve all this time.

The discerning old timer sat there, waiting for the singer's reaction, but Pacer was still attempting to digest the contract's contents. Was Henderson actually appointing him to drive the Cadillac to Memphis? Did he mean that he was to oversee its transportation by other means?

'I can see this contract I want you to sign comes with some bewilderment on your face, giving you no prior information about what it truly entails, so I'll explain. Then we'll both know if you want to sign it or not,' Willard ventured.

'When someone gets old and decrepit, just like you're seeing me, you get to thinking not about the future. There's not much incentive in doing that, Pacer. What really matters when you come to the end of the trail is: how clear is my conscience? How many people did I hurt along the way? Could I put any of it right before I die? But I can't turn the clock back, most of those I remember doing wrong to are now dead or like me, close to judgement day.

'I've been thinkin' for some time, even before I got ill, wondering what will happen when I'm gone, who'd take care of Fleet? That's when I got the idea of returning her to her rightful place. Graceland. The only chance of me apologising to Elvis will be at the Pearly Gates. But I could put it to him better if he got the Cadillac back in one piece, like when he bought her in '56.'

The more Henderson was talking, the more impatient Pacer became, wanting to know whether or not he wanted him to drive it back to Memphis, something he wasn't keen on doing. She looked too exquisite, too vulnerable, to be responsible for her safe delivery.

'Excuse me, Mr Henderson, for stopping you there. I've got the feeling that you want me to take the wheel and drive the Cadillac half way across America. Is that right?'

'You're dead right I do, son. I have that much faith in you, otherwise we wouldn't be talking right now. You wouldn't even be here.' He produced a 22 carat gold fountain pen and waved it in front of Pacer. He gave a deep sigh, no doubt it was filled with doubts.

'What are you waiting for?' simpered Henderson, leaning over, offering the pen. 'Too big a job to take on? Hey, kid, I reckon you're wanting to be paid extra,' he chuckled. 'Sign it, son. Sign it for me, sign it for Elvis, sign it for yourself. You won't regret it.'

The library sounded more like a graveyard full of headstones than books. Pacer pondered whether to take the pen or take a deferral. He took the pen and was about to sign the contract when...

'Wait, before you sign, I got a checklist that needs promising. Don't even think of breaking the speed limit over there. Keep her under 50mph. She's an old girl and remember, you do this on your own, no hitch-hikers and no leavin' her on her own where you can't keep an eye on her. I reckon it's gonna be around 1,000 miles from the docks in New York to Memphis. She'll be shipped over to the States. If I had my way you'd be sleeping with her while crossing the Atlantic. Sign here, kid. It won't make you a star, but you'll certainly be rich.'

Pacer duly signed the document and Willard added his signature before both signed the second copy. Pacer leaned over the desk and they shook hands on the deal. But Henderson hadn't quite finished.

'Just one more thing, young man,' he said, quizzically. 'Just out of curiosity, you being an authority on the history of Elvis, as you proved on that TV show and you being a kind of mechanic, do you know much about the Cadillac, the specifications side of her?'

'Well,' replied Pacer, his eyes lighting up, 'I was good and ready for that question but they didn't even mention the car, which I thought was a little strange, it being a significant feature of Elvis's fame.'

Henderson leaned back, relaxing into the plumped up satin pillows provided on his wheelchair, like a stern magistrate holding court, watery-eyed and judgemental. 'Tell me what you know,' he asked. 'Take your time. Ain't no-one perfect. It won't change a thing.'

Pacer looked upbeat. 'Okay,' he began. 'I learned a lot from my dad, him being into car engines and stuff. He was a big Presley fan and would have loved to have owned that Cadillac. Anyway, here goes,' leaning a little forward in his chair, thinking the old man's hearing could compromise the challenge he faced.

'Series 62 Sedan, 250 horsepower V8 engine. Wheelbase 1,498 inches. Pushbutton automatic windshield wipers. Automatic choke. 4 door Sedan, seating six. Dual exhausts. Length, 5,495 mm. Weight, 15,989kg. Heating and ventilation system. Power brakes. Power electric seats. Power electric windows. Air conditioning. Automatic headlamp dipper. Intimidating teeth-grinding grille, giving it a she-devil-like quality, toned down by the pink paintwork...'

Henderson had fallen fast asleep.

Pacer didn't want to wake him up, looking so peaceful in slumber. He looked at his watch. It was getting late, time for him to be on his way. Henderson hadn't said anything about what arrangements were to be made regarding when he was expected to leave for the States.

Perhaps falling asleep had not given him the chance.

Leaving the library, he went in search for one of Henderson's carers. The room he eerily called his departure lounge was deserted. However, he caught up with Dino Rosetti as he was about to climb the hallway's staircase. The chauffeur turned, hearing Pacer's footsteps echoing through the hall.

'Oh, 'ello. You okay?' offered Dino, surprised that his boss wasn't with him. 'Where Mr Henderson. Where he go?' his voice raised with concern.

Pacer quickly responded. 'He's fine. I left him fast asleep in the library. We'd been looking at the Cadillac, where he's stored it, and then we had a long talk afterwards. He left his wheelchair for a while and it must have drained him.'

'Si. He ready for bed. He very sick man. He worry me.'

'Yes,' said Pacer, 'and such a gentleman. He's had an amazing life, hasn't he?'

'Si, it also very sad. He tell you about his wife and son? They die in avalanche.'

'Yes,' sighed Pacer. 'It's heartbreaking. I feel very sorry for him, having all that he's achieved, this beautiful place and not having his family to share it with. All this luxury, yet in a way his loss has left him feeling poorer than a church mouse. It's very sad.'

'Si, it also very late, you stay here tonight. Yes? Mr Henderson, he want to say goodbye in morning. He not say goodbye now. Nurse Tanya maka you supper, then you sleep. It like 5 star hotel bedroom.'

Pacer mulled it over in his head. It was a fair old run back to Hammersmith. He'd already more or less completed a day's work at the garage and he felt tired. What tempted him in accepting Dino's offer was the opportunity to speak to Henderson in the morning. There was a lot more to be discussed than the specifications of the Cadillac. Questions like, when was it all going to kick off? If Henderson wanted it to coincide with Elvis's anniversary, August 16, three months ahead from now, was it really necessary to wait that long? Considering the state he was in, he could be dead before then.

Dino hadn't exaggerated when he said that the bedroom was like a 5 star hotel. In fact it wouldn't have been an exaggeration if he had said 10 star. Apart from Dino's and Tanya's own separate bedrooms, most of the other nine bedrooms in the Manor had been mothballed years ago. There once was a time, before tragedy had cast its shadow on the property, Willard had held fabulous parties and celebrations there. His friends and business associates would often stay overnight, some of them sleeping in the same sumptuous surroundings that Pacer was now experiencing, laying awake in a four poster bed in an oak-panelled bedroom complete with antique furnishings, a chandelier hanging from a high, oak-beamed ceiling and paintings of what seemed like ancestral-looking characters, going back hundreds of years, none of them being of dark skin. Paintings left by the previous owner who had died in the same bed that Pacer now occupied.

It would have been fair to say that Pacer, although tired, wasn't keen on turning the chandelier lights off in such atmospheric, ghostlike conditions. Nevertheless, he bravely did so, his ears pricked in silence that was deafening. Just as he was about to drop off, he heard moaning and the sound of thumps and scratching noises coming from the corridor outside the bedroom door, before suddenly ceasing.

Stiffening, Pacer stared into the darkness, his senses revving. 'Who's there? Who's that?' he breathed. There was no answer. Laying there, his mind conjured up a list of ghostly scenarios until his eyes slowly fluttered into unconsciousness. Suddenly they burst open. Something or someone had hit the door with some force and Pacer wasn't having any more of it!

Sliding out of bed, he crept towards the door. Switching the chandelier lights on, he slowly opened it. It creaked like a scalded cat. He peered into the semi-darkness of the corridor now lit by the doorway, but there was nothing there, only silence. Just as he was about to close the door, an entity came rushing along the corridor, jumping up at him.

It was Rex, wagging his tail.

Every night, the dog was given licence to walk the Manor, on the prowl for mice or any other vermin that shouldn't be there. True to his breed, anything he caught would be presented to Mrs Dale, the housekeeper, when she arrived for work first thing in the morning.

Pacer slept well after his friendly encounter with the midnight marauder. He was gently woken by the swish of heavy curtains being drawn open by none other than sexy Tanya Brooks, wearing an ivory silk dressing gown, shimmering in morning sun. She turned away from the window and headed towards the four-poster bed and the young man, naked beneath the duvet but for his Armani boxer shorts. On the bedside table sat a tray laden with tea, three rounds of toast and jar of marmalade.

'Wakey, wakey,' she smiled. 'Hope you slept well, and Rex didn't come visiting you during the night. We don't get many visitors, and if he sniffed that you were here...'

'He sniffed, that's for sure,' interrupted Pacer, getting comfortable, sitting up in bed, bare chested, a St. Christopher hanging from his neck. 'He kept me awake last night, scratching the door. I thought it was a bloody ghost. When I went and took a look, he had a mouse in his mouth.'

'That doesn't surprise me,' laughed Tanya, perching herself on the edge of the bed, near the singer. 'We have lots of field mice in this neck of the woods. Now you know why they're called Retrievers.'

If Pacer looked lethargic before Tanya settled on the bed,

it now seemed like a bedspring had smacked his bum!

Prior to entering the bedroom, the nurse had dabbed her wrist with Eau de Cologne, not that Pacer hadn't noticed.

Unusually for him, the 32-year-old bombshell made him feel, if not uncomfortable, a bit wary. Where did Dino fit into all this? Were they a couple? Those Italians can be hot-headed, he thought.

'Erm... thanks for the supper last night, Tanya. That wine Dino uncorked was really smooth. I must thank him for it before I shoot off.'

'Oh, that won't be possible.' she enthused. 'He got up early. He's taken the Rolls into town. It needs a service.'

Yes, like you, thought the singer.

Tanya moved closer, gazing at the pendant. 'What's that around your neck?' she purred, smoothing the gold ingot bearing the image of a saint sensitively with her fingers.

'Oh, it's St. Christopher,' he smiled. 'He's the Patron Saint of Travellers. I wear it for good luck. It's like he protects those who wear it.'

'I see,' Tanya teased, stroking the length of the chain hanging from his nape. 'Well, how far are you willing to travel?'

'How far?' he breathed. 'All the way, baby...'

An hour later, Pacer was back in the library again, chatting with Henderson, discussing the finer preparations regarding his forthcoming journey to America. In his view, the old man was being too idealistic, timing his arrival in Memphis on the same date as the anniversary, August 16. Pacer suggested that he be given more leeway, arriving at least a few days earlier, shacking up somewhere until the big day arrived, parking the Cadillac at Graceland's gates, or close by, before handing the car keys over to whoever's on security duty. Willard had already composed a letter revealing everything about the history of the Fleetwood; who he was, why he had stolen it, how he regretted it happening. But now, with his life ebbing, seeking forgiveness, absolution would make him a new man in the next world. Elvis's world. He told Pacer, the letter and the car's bill of sale proving its authenticity should also accompany the keys, and that an evidential phone video of the transaction must be taken, with the Cadillac visually appearing in it, to be wired to him immediately.

Henderson leaned forward in his wheelchair, his hand reaching over his desk, offering it to Pacer. 'Okay, son,' he sighed. 'All for the time being. Off you go and don't go changing your mind. I'm 85 years old and in a wheelchair but It don't matter, these wheels can fly, kid. You won't escape,' he wisecracked.

'I won't let you down, Mr Henderson,' said Pacer, heading out of the library. 'To be honest, I can't wait to get behind that steering wheel, one million pounds, or no million pounds...!'

The garage doors slowly opened and the prestigious Cadillac kept inside for so many years, saw the light of day again. Rolling out into the blazing August sunshine, the first stop on her epic journey was the forecourt, where Henderson, Tanya and Dino were waiting outside the Manor's entrance with Rex. The small party had already said their good-byes to Pacer, behind the wheel of the Fleetwood, wearing a cowboy hat, the picture of happiness.

Willard Henderson, on the other hand, looked sad as a beau at a railway station saying goodbye to his sweetheart for the last time.

His final exchange, his voice choking, he called out, 'See that you drive the old girl up to those gates without so much as a scratch on her,' he warned. 'I don't want Elvis gettin' sore with me when we meet up again on the other side. Those other kind of gates.'

The singer nodded. With a toot of its horn the fabulous-looking machine headed along the driveway and through the main gates. Travelling light, Pacer's only possessions, a hold-all full of spare clothes, hairdryer and other essential items for the journey. On the back seat, his precious Gibson in its case. He was heading for Southampton Docks; unknown to him, a road trip fraught with a thousand stings. Maybe a bit of an exaggeration, but fraught all the same.

A mile along the way and the Cadillac entered the dense forest, only the second time for her to do so, having been holed up in the Manor all those years. Although Pacer had travelled through it a number of times, he always felt relieved when it was over. The wilderness of ancient, gnarled trees, like a scene from The Wizard Of Oz, unpleasant. But it was a different story this time. The summer sun, filtering through the leafy canopy, created spots of sunlight intermitted with the softly shaded lane ahead of him. The Fleetwood was only travelling around 20mph. but the dappled foliage whizzing by seemed to double its speed and that suited Pacer, aware that there was no mobile signal, only accessible once he'd left the forest.

All seemed well, until...

The brakes were hit too late. Too late to avoid the rabbit, now probably dead, too late to stop. Whatever damage had been caused by the animal, it would have been minimal, considering the speed of the car and there was no chance of doing a U turn to the Manor, not that the narrow lane would have allowed, trying to explain a dent in the bumper to an irate Henderson. Pacer was on a one-way ticket whatever scrapes may be ahead of him, or the Cadillac.

After leaving the forest, the singer stopped and checked

for any damage. It was nothing to write home about, or in this case, the Manor. It was insignificant enough to be barely noticeable, the dent on the underside of the chrome bumper.

It had taken over two hours to drive to Southampton Docks via the M25 and M3. Apart from the incident with the rabbit, all was well. It would take ten days transit in the purpose-built ships that sailed every week to New York. Henderson had given Pacer a choice. He could accompany the Cadillac on the ship, experiencing the life of a seafarer, with all the privileges the ship could offer: first-class cabin, à la carte menu, alcoholic drinks, generously paid for by Willard Henderson. Or he could fly to New York in no time and meet up with the Fleetwood.

Pacer made up his mind, also in no time. Ten days at sea. Remembering the old seafaring adage about a sailor having a girl in every port, he'd figured maybe he'd get lucky, having a girl mid-Atlantic! Anyway, he never felt comfortable, wedged in a metal tube, the only view through that little window, the plane's wing-tip and fluffy clouds. Worse still, having to join the queue in the aisle, bursting for a pee, looking composed, cool and imperturbable, nonchalantly whistling to oneself while almost losing bowel control, along with the waterworks.

Having thoroughly enjoyed his ten days at sea, with all the trimmings on board, Pacer was now behind the wheel of the Fleetwood again, driving out of New York's harbour and looking very much the American stereotype. Levi jacket and jeans, cowboy hat and cowboy boots, sunglasses predictably perched on his forehead. The only thing missing on his tee-shirt: "When In Rome".

FIVE

I CAN'T HELP FALLING IN LOVE

Driving out of the city was his real first challenge. Manoeuvring through heavy traffic with such a massive limousine was a hair-raising experience, especially with Henderson's warning ringing in his ears.

'See that you get that old girl to the gates of Graceland, without so much of a scratch.' The 'old girl' had already been scarred by a scared rabbit and if the old man could see her now, bumper to bumper, surrounded by blaring car horns, stuck in a traffic jam, tempers rising higher than New York's humidity, he'd have blown a bigger gasket than the car close by, steam spurting from its hood.

The traffic was now on the move again and according to his sat-nav, Highway 78, Turnpike was up ahead. Pacer could leave behind the stress and turmoil of the bustling, buzzing metropolis which to paraphrase Frank Sinatra, in the frankest of ways, "The city that never sleeps."

With 1,100 miles ahead of him, and New York behind, the Fleetwood's chaperone abided by one of the rules Henderson had laid down. No faster than 45-50 mph. It meant cruising along in the slow lane. Pacer switched on the venerable radio that had been in the Cadillac since '56, tuning into the first station he came across. Taylor Swift's 'Ready for it?' hit the airwaves, clear as a bell. Pacer began humming along with the catchy tune, but the station's signal broke up and she was lost.

Undeterred, he tried another station. Country singer LeAnn Rimes came through with 'How Do I Live', loud and clear. But within ten seconds, the song fizzled out. Pacer put the blame on the antique radio, giving it a tap with his hand. It seemed to work. Out popped Lady Gaga's 'Poker Face', but that soon went the same way as the other female singers.

Becoming exasperated, he shouted, 'This relic doesn't even have a bloody cassette player.'

He was about to switch the radio off when suddenly it blasted out Chuck Berry's classic rock and roll number, 'Maybellene', almost loud enough to be heard where he was heading: Memphis.

After 'Maybellene' had finished, the radio switched off by itself which got Pacer thinking that the Cadillac may have been responsible for not allowing female singers any airplay. After all, anyone who had watched Stephen King's horror movie, Christine, proved that jealousy can be absorbed in many different guises.

Cruising along in his automobile, Chuck Berry's lyrics still clinging to his ears, Pacer's thoughts turned towards Nashville, the heart of country music. Once his mission had been achieved, flying back to London on the first plane was definitely a no-no. He'd never been to that great city where dreams came true, producing some of the greatest country singers, musicians ever. Memphis was too close, too near, for him to turn his back on its famous neighbour, the reason he'd brought his guitar along. Who knew what it may lead to? He'd contest, hang around the bars, getting up, singing a few songs, hoping to outshine other performers and that some producer might be interested in signing him to a record label. He'd seen it happening in the movies, what did he have to lose? It was worth a try.

Driving from New York to Memphis at an average speed

of 65mph. it would take around sixteen hours to arrive. With the Cadillac doing around 50mph. it would reach the city in an additional five. Although Pacer was a rally driver and used to being behind the wheel for many hours, this was a bridge too far for him to contemplate attempting.

A rumbling stomach was the sign for him to look out for a roadside eatery. It wasn't long before he pulled into Wendy's Restaurant, where fate would deal him a companion for the rest of the journey, even though Henderson had insisted there were to be no hitchhikers involved.

Illegal exhaust emissions spewing from a packed Greyhound leaving the service station stung the eyes of the 21-year-old girl kneeling on the sun-hot tarmac. She watched it roar away back onto the highway, taking her suitcase with it. Sobbing, she rose to her feet clutching her handbag, desperately waving, trying to get the bus driver's attention. It was futile. To make things worse, the poor girl accidentally spilled the contents of her handbag onto the ground.

The attractive, flaxen-haired lost soul fell to her knees again, gathering the items scattered over the ground and putting them into the bag, her hands shaking. She had been in the rest room, addressing her makeup, in conversation with another traveller, losing count of the time. Dressed in a crop top and denim shorts, all her other clothes were in her suitcase now on the road to somewhere. She cast a sorry-looking figure in the busy car park, vehicles passing close by. Some far too close for comfort.

Her scream, loud as a car horn, turned heads as she looked up, fell backwards onto her bum, horror-stricken by the sight of the teeth-grinding, she-devil grille of a pink Cadillac almost touching her white trainered feet.

Pacer poked his head from its window, adjusting his

sunglasses, tipping back his cowboy hat.

'Hey,' he smiled. You okay? Take an overdose, its far less messy.'

Rising to her feet, eyes flashing with contempt, she protested. 'Oh, yeah. Maybe scaring me to death would be even cleaner! You some kind of time traveller? That relic should be in a museum,' she jeered. 'Maybe you think you're Elton John. Huh, same lousy accent!'

Pacer was taken aback by her feisty attitude, but also impressed by it. 'Aw, c'mon,' he declared. 'I was just trying to protect you from all those cars running over you. Chill out, saw you chasing after that coach. Looks like you've been abandoned.'

'Oh, get lost,' she replied, turning on her heel, heading in the direction of the restaurant. 'You and your gay Cadillac.'

She was some beauty, and the randy singer wasn't giving up, steering the Fleetwood alongside her, his voice expressing sympathy in its tone. 'Look, I'm sorry if I startled you. Can I help? I'm heading for Memphis, the same way as the bus. I can give you a lift to where you're going, unless you want to wait for another bus to come along.'

The offer seemed to work, at least she stopped in her tracks.

'I got delayed in the rest room and the bus left without me, taking my suitcase with it,' she groaned. 'That goddamn impatient driver, I could wring his neck.' With that, she disappeared into the restaurant, moaning, 'I need a strong coffee.'

Pacer followed her, like a dog on heat, but not before he'd parked the Fleetwood where he could still see her from inside the restaurant. He found the distressed traveller sitting at a table near a window, where he could keep an eye on the old girl.

Quietly sitting opposite her, trusting she wouldn't object to his presence by interfering with her lamenting, he said. 'Hey, cheer up. I'll contact the bus company on my mobile. They can arrange for the bus driver to drop off your suitcase at the next roadside service station. I'll take you there after I've had a bite to eat. I'm starving, been on the road all day after leaving the docks in New York.'

The mention of the docks seemed to strike an inquisitive chord with the girl. Composing herself, she said, 'Are you saying what I think you're saying – you're English? You crossed the Atlantic with that Cadillac out there?'

'Yes,' sighed Pacer. 'Now, if you tell me your name, I'll tell you mine, then I'll tell you all about that pink Cadillac you christened gay.' Turning in his seat, he signalled for a waiter.

His opposite number looked a little less tense, now that there was a good chance of being reunited with the suitcase, and her opposite number seemed to be a genuine guy, plus very good looking. If he was gay, what an ache it would be, she sighed.

After Pacer had caught the eye of a waitress, he turned and asked. 'So, are you going to tell me your name? Let me guess,' he said, quizzically. 'An intense name like Rebecca or Rachel. Potent.'

'Those names may be potent to you, but you're way out,' she replied, melancholically. 'Sorry to disappoint, but my name is Annabelle... Annabelle Chimes. Most people I know call me Belle.'

Pacer responded with a warm smile.

'Okay,' she sighed.' I can see it in your face. Just don't say it,' she warned.

'See what? Say what?' he protested, frowning uneasily.

'Belle,' she emphasised, staring at him, poker-faced. 'Belle... Belle Chimes.'

Their discussion was fortunately interrupted by the

waitress, blandly asking, 'Are you ready to order now?'

Pacer grinned at the waitress, but it was a double entendre, meant to cover his funny bone, hoping it wouldn't ring a bell with Belle. 'Yes please,' he said, before asking his silent companion if she was also going to eat.

'No, not for me,' she said, leaning forward. 'I'll just have a coffee. When I do eat, I go vegan. Can't bear eating anything with pleading eyes, thank you very much. Meat is for savages.'

'Everyone to their own taste,' came the reply. Pacer took off his aviators. 'I reckon I'll go for my usual juicy steak. Rib-eye, rare, with all the trimmings,' he teased. 'Oh, by the way, I'm Pacer Burton. Forgive me, but I'm mercilessly hungry.'

Pacer's mobile rang as he waited for the meal to arrive. It was Willard Henderson. Back at the Manor, Pacer had been dismayed to see how much the cancer had taken its toll on the old man. It seemed a miracle that he'd managed to leave his sick bed to send him on his way.

'Hello, you out of those docks yet?' Henderson's voice sounded thinner and rougher than a sheet of sandpaper. 'On that road now?' he gasped, having temporally removed his oxygen mask.

'Hello. Mr Henderson. I hope you're okay to talk. Your breathing...'

'I'll ask you again, boy. How far?' he interrupted, impatiently.

'Oh, we're about 300 miles out of New York. Just taking a break at a service station.'

'We're? What do you mean by 'we're'? You got someone with you? I warned you...'

'No way,' lied Pacer, his voice, now pitched a couple of tones higher. 'I know what you said about hitchhikers.'

Pumped up with painkillers, his speech, laboured and

slurring, Henderson dismayed Pacer when he said, 'Where are you? You should be outside Graceland, handing over those keys.'

'No, Mr Henderson. I… I just told you. I'm having a break, stopping for a meal. It's the first day on the road. There's a long way to go, another 800 miles.'

'Oh, yeah? Well, how come you've stopped to eat?' he grizzled. 'Tell me your itinerary, from when you started. What town are you in?'

Disturbed by his almost incoherent ranting, Pacer gently explained the travel plan, something he and Henderson had gone over many times prior to him leaving Southampton.

'I'm not stopping in any town, Mr Henderson, I'm staying on the highway, all the way to Memphis. I left New York Docks early this morning, about 8am eastern time. I sailed from Southampton on August 2nd. Today is the 13th, and all being well, I'll be in Memphis by the 15th. In time for Elvis's anniversary, the 16th.'

'Hell,' spluttered the old man. 'Why didn't you tell me all this before? It's all new to me. Listen. I'm out of oxygen… my breathin'…' The line went dead.

While waiting for his steak, Pacer contacted the Greyhound Bus Company regarding the suitcase. Arrangements were made to collect it at the next roadside service station. During the meal, the singer felt obliged to tell Belle all about the mission. In response, he learned that his passenger was visiting relatives, her aunt and uncle. This time going it alone without her parents tagging along on a summer vacation, away from the stresses of working in a Manhattan bank.

Leaving the restaurant, Pacer refuelled the Fleet and rejoined the highway, aiming to put another 100 miles behind it, taking up two more hours of the long day.

Keeping them company, the funky old radio, seemingly

with a mind of its own, played Chuck Berry and Paul Simon records which appealed to both parties. 'No Particular Place To Go' and 'Graceland'.

Singing along with the music, they had only travelled around twenty miles when their voices suddenly trailed off. Up ahead, parked on the side of the road, was the Greyhound bus. A number of its passengers loitered nearby. Some were using their suitcases as seats, fanning themselves to stay cool.

Pacer pulled in behind the bus. 'I don't know what's going on here,' he said to Belle, getting out of the Cadillac, 'but your suitcase may be amongst the others on the side of the road.'

He found the bus driver removing more cases from the cargo hold. After a short conversation, the driver handed over the girl's suitcase.

Striding back to the car, Pacer opened the rear door and dropped the case on the seat before getting into his own. 'Broken down,' he explained. 'Happy now?' He nodded at the suitcase. 'They're waiting for another coach to pick them up.'

'Thanks for rescuing it,' she smiled, adding, 'I'm not surprised it broke down, all those exhaust fumes belching from it as it left the car park.'

'Well,' said Pacer, 'now that you've got your suitcase back, I won't be dropping you off at the next service station. How much further do you intend going, where do your relatives live?'

'Oh, it's a small town, about a hundred miles further down the road. Just a few miles off this highway.'

'Okay, I'm happy to take you there, no problem.'

Belle didn't say no to the kind offer. In fact, her face glowed with happiness.

The incident back at the service station, where the Cadillac crept up on her with such intimidation, seemed far behind. Belle was warming towards Pacer more with every mile they covered, feeling safe in his company. Cruising along, she began appreciating the Cadillac's credentials, the car's uniqueness and past history. It pleased Pacer when she began calling the limousine Fleet, rather than the Cadillac, or the Fleetwood.

So far, she was behaving like a true thoroughbred, giving no hint of her age. Henderson's advice to keep her speed no higher than 50mph, seemed to be paying off. They had another 20 miles to reach their destination, according to the sat-nav. Pacer suddenly turned off the radio, still churning out rock and roll. Ahead of them, the sun was setting and the singer's love of the natural world became evident.

'Hey, Belle,' he enthused. 'Just look at that sun going down, it's more than beautiful, it's breathtaking.'

'Yeah,' smiled Belle, gazing through the windshield, 'you get some real beauties the further west you go, especially this time of year. One thing's for sure, it's a sign of what tomorrow will bring. Red sky at night, shepherd's delight, meaning sunshine all the way. A dreamy sunset.'

Pacer had been driving for almost eight hours flat, covering 400 miles since leaving New York. When he yawned, Belle asked where he was going to sleep that night.

'Have you planned on stopping overnight? You're not gonna carry on, surely? You look beat.'

'No way, I've had enough driving for one day. There's bound to be a comfortable hotel pillow to rest my head on, somewhere in town.'

'I got an idea,' said Belle, turning in her seat to face him. 'There's no need to drive into town looking for somewhere. When we leave the highway, we hit the road to where I'm staying. On the way, there's a swell place called Quincy's

Bar and Guest House. The guy who owns it is a great bull of a man with a long beard,' she laughed. 'ZZ Top got nothing on it – you'll see.'

'Sounds good to me,' said Pacer. 'Let's hope they got a spare room for me, and close to where I can leave the Cadillac.'

'I'm sure Fleet will be okay,' she smiled. 'I've never known any trouble there, it's a respectable establishment. You won't see any trouble in Quincy's, it's a real cosy place. The owner is a gentle giant but he won't stand for any of that kinda nonsense, no sir. Peace and love has always been Quincy's reputation. I've known him for years, calling in whenever I'm down here. They've got a resident Country and Western band. Sometimes I get up and give a song... not that I'm any good,' she sighed.

Leaving the highway, they headed down a dark country road, with Belle still singing Quincy's praises. Then, there it was, as she had described, laying back off the road. A long, single storey building made of stone and wood, its lights ablaze. Over the entrance, a large neon sign. 'Quincy's Bar'.

SIX

GOOD ROCKIN' TONIGHT

There seemed no unoccupied parking spaces, so Pacer pulled up quite near to the entrance, aware that he wasn't going to stay long before taking Belle home. The muffled sounds of bass guitar and drums resonated through thick stone walls, smothering the sounds of other instruments being played.

Before walking towards the entrance, Pacer lifted his guitar and luggage off the rear seat and placed them in the enormous trunk. 'Better safe than sorry,' he told Belle, 'though I won't be here long.'

Locking the trunk, he remarked on the band's volume. 'One thing, they're not too loud. I'll be able to get some sleep, even if they're at it until after midnight. How many in the band, Belle?'

'They're a five-piece,' she said. 'They have a violinist, but you won't be hearing anything classical coming from this lot.'

Reaching the entrance, the singer looked over his shoulder, concerned. 'I hope I've done the right thing, leaving her alone out here,' Henderson's voice visiting him: 'Don't leave her for one minute. Sleep with her if you have to.'

'C'mon,' enthused Belle. 'Lets go in, see what Quincy's got to say about staying. I don't know about you, but I won't say no to a cold beer while we're here.' She eagerly threw open the door.

The amplification that met them was enough to pin their ears back. Pacer's hope for a reasonable quiet night's sleep was now splintered by the band's version of Charlie Daniel's, 'The Devil Went Down To Georgia'.

The five-piece were performing on a small stage directly opposite the entrance. It was a miracle that Pacer's Stetson hadn't gone the same way as his ears. They were deafening enough, even for the devil.

The bar-room was heaving with customers partying as if it was New Year's Eve. Belle admitted later on, that she had never seen it as full. Taking Pacer's hand, their first physical contact, she turned left heading for the bar at the end of the long room where Quincy and two of his staff were serving. Making their way, they had to negotiate around tables overloaded with cans and beer bottles. Country-dressed drinkers sat there, obviously in for the long haul.

No line dancing in Quincy's Bar tonight. It would have been too mild for those gathered on the dance floor near the stage, considering the kind of heavy Country music the band were knocking out.

Making it to the end of the packed room, both travellers had to fight their way through the crush of customers at the bar. The air was permeated with Budweiser and other alcoholic beverages, some of it spilled accidentally onto the floor in a mayhem of thirst.

Belle's description of Quincy was no exaggeration. Through the hubbub of noise around her, Belle yelled to get the proprietor's attention. 'Hey, Quincy!' she waved, 'come here!'

Quincy nodded in acknowledgement before taking a customer's money and slamming it in the till. The exceedingly large figure tossed a bar towel over his shoulder and wended his way along the bar towards them. Had the bar not been in the way, he would have probably greeted

Belle with a bear hug. Instead, his voice deeper than Barry White's double chin, he hollered, 'Well, I'll be... What a surprise, girl. Ain't seen hide or hair of you for, let's see now... must be a year ago. I have to say it, Belle, once in a year ain't enough for a pretty girl like you.'

Reaching over, Belle affectionately tugged at his bushy bird-nest-beard. 'Ah, that's kind of you, Quincy,' she gushed. 'Listen, my English friend here, he's looking for a place to sleep tonight. Can you accommodate him?'

The grey-haired, ponytailed, larger-than-life character slapped the towel onto the bar and shook his head side to side. 'Girl,' he sniffed, 'havin' known you since you bin' a child, your uncle and aunt bringing you in here in summertime, a glass of chilled lemonade, I have to tell you. This here place was booked up for accommodation months ago. Quincy's full of Elvis fans, all of them on a pilgrimage to Graceland, 45 years since he bin' dead. All the hotels in town are fully booked for the anniversary. Sorry Belle, your friend here's gonna have to sleep under the stars tonight, unless he can stay with your relatives.'

Quincy looked genuinely frustrated, having to refuse her plea. 'Hey, you young uns, you both look as though you could appreciate a cold beer each,' gesturing to one of the barmen, attempting to change the subject.

'Oh, okay, I understand,' sighed Belle, lowering her head, looking disappointed, thinking Quincy may have a change of heart. But instead, Quincy nodded at the singer.

'Who's this good lookin' kid. I ain't seen him with you before now, Belle?'

Belle held Pacer's waist. 'We got talking on the way down here from New York,' she said, before introducing them to each other. 'He's driving a pink Cadillac from England to Memphis. Pacer is a singer, a tribute act. A big fan of Elvis.'

'Yeah,' flashed Quincy. 'Well, yeah, come to think of it,

76

he sure resembles the King.

'Why don't you two get up on that stage and maybe sing a song together, something you both know. You know how much everyone here love your singin', Belle,' he coaxed.

Never one to turn down the chance of getting up on stage with a band behind him, Pacer got shot down just as he was about to speak. Belle had caught the glint of enthusiasm in his eyes. 'I dont think so,' she spluttered, choking on a mouthful of cold beer. 'No way! Not in front of this noisy crowd!'

'Aw, c'mon, Belle,' smiled Quincy. 'You can see they're all in a good mood. The more people the merrier!' He looked at Pacer. 'What you reckon, son. You up for it? She can sing real good, but she doesn't seem to know it.'

'Yeah, I don't mind getting up, if Belle thinks it's okay. I know a load of songs but it has to be one we both know!'

'Are you kidding,' wailed Belle. 'I only know about six songs. No chance!'

'Hold it, hold it,' drawled Quincy. 'Calm down. It's only a suggestion. No big deal,' he sniffed, meaning he hadn't given up. 'What's that Donna Summer number I heard you sing with one of my customers, last time you were in here?'

"Hot Stuff',' offered Belle, trying her best to sound uninterested.

Pacer was quick to respond. 'I know that one. It's a classic. C'mon Belle, let's kick ass, as they say around here!'

'Done deal!' whooped Quincy, turning on his heel, leaving the bar heading for the stage.

He'd left an extremely attractive individual standing next to Pacer, ordering a brandy, reminding him that a vulnerable pink Cadillac was parked outside, hoping it would get her off the hook.

Pacer, being Pacer, eager to get up on stage and sing wasn't listening. The band had stopped playing and Quincy was talking to the lead guitarist and pointing towards the bar. Seconds later, he beckoned for them to come to the stage. Belle finished off her brandy, gave a deep sigh and followed the singer, weaving her way through the crowd, looking nervous as a lamb.

While Pacer was discussing the song with the musicians, Belle approached Quincy, asking him if he wouldn't mind checking out the Cadillac while they were on stage as they hadn't intended staying this long.

'I'll do that, right now,' he chuckled. 'Not that there's any need to. This is Quincy's, not San Quentin, girl.'

Meanwhile, up on stage, the good-looking duo gathered around the microphone stand, ready to kick-off.

At least we look dressed for the occasion, thought Belle. If all else falls apart.

On the contrary, choosing 'Hot Stuff' for their performance had nailed it. Afterwards, the bar room erupted, exploding with applause, whooping and crying out for more. Both singers stood there with fixed smiles, looking at each other in disbelief at such a reaction. Belle made the first move. She couldn't get off the stage quick enough!

'Oh, gee. Thanks, everybody,' smiling nervously into the mic. 'We'd like to sing another one but we don't know any more.'

Pacer backed her up, leaning into the mic. 'For the record folks, this is the first time we've sung together. In fact, we never met each other until this morning. Honest truth.'

A great round of applause and cheering filled the chocablock room. Still, the smiling duo would have willingly shared it with Quincy. While they were singing, his mighty arm was in a vice-like headlock around the neck of a robbing thief he'd caught prising the Cadillac's trunk with a screwdriver. Later, he would vehemently protest his innocence when the law arrived, but right now he was weeping with fear, the prisoner of a 20 stone angry bar owner.

Still adrenalised after their performance, the singer soon came down to earth when Belle told him she had asked Quincy to check on Fleet, but he hadn't returned. Pacer immediately headed for the doorway, anxiousness compounded by speed.

Still holding on to his captive, Quincy shouted when Pacer appeared. 'Unlock the car door! I want this piece of shit in the back so I can call the cops. I caught him breaking into the trunk!'

Pacer obliged, keeping an eye on the scruffy juvenile while Quincy was on the phone. Now they had an audience around them, including Belle who watched Pacer examining the damage done to the locking mechanism of the trunk, courtesy of the screwdriver. It wouldn't close properly, so it wasn't the best of endings to what had been a free-and-easy day for the Cadillac.

After the police had taken the thief away and things had calmed down, Pacer managed to close the trunk but was unable to lock it, so the guitar and luggage were laid out on the rear seat again. The pair were on their way, heading for Belle's relatives a few miles further down the road. Pacer had no intention of asking if he could shack up with them for the night. Instead, he planned on making his way back to Quincy's and sleeping in the Cadillac. He and Belle had arranged to say their farewells the following morning. Although desperately tired, predictably, he didn't sleep well.

The pink Cadillac had been driven away from Crighton Manor without so much as a speck of dust to be seen on her hood, thanks to Dino Rosetti's pristine polishing. What would Henderson have thought of her now, after suffering two misfortunes? Dust would have been welcome.

Belle, prophesying, 'red sky at night, shepherd's delight',

would hark, 'blue sky in morning, sunshine a'calling' now. Another glorious day. Idealistically, a cockerel giving full delivery would have caused Pacer to open his eyes. Instead, the sharp rapping on the Cadillac's window.

'Wake up! Wake up, Pacer!' It was Belle peering through the glass. 'Quincy's got breakfast on the go. Wake up!'

And wake up he did, once he caught the smell of bacon, eggs and beans hitting his senses. Lifting himself out of the car, stretching his aching joints, the drowsy singer yawned. He was surprised to see that two breakfasts had been laid out on a table under a colourful parasol, courtesy of a thoughtful, generous-minded Quincy.

The gentle giant was standing near the bar's entrance, smiling broadly, bar towel slung over his shoulder. 'Mornin' Elvis,' he quipped. 'Should have slept under the stars, like I suggested. You wouldn't be as stiff.'

'I'll remember that, next time,' groaned Pacer, sitting down at the table with Belle. 'If you've a spare bed going.'

'I'll make sure of it,' responded Quincy, leaving the couple to enjoy their al fresco breakfast.

Belle had come along to say goodbye, not to have breakfast on the house. She'd already eaten a cereal, but Quincy had insisted, promising a rationed serving.

Tucking into his meal, Pacer suggested she accompany him to Memphis. She looked even more beautiful, having taken the trouble to give that impression. Her make-up was immaculate, and she was wearing a halter style summer dress, showing off her ample shoulders. Pacer looked besotted.

'I'd love to,' she smiled, 'I really would. I've never been to Memphis, and visiting Graceland would be fantastic but I don't think my uncle and aunt would be too keen, as you can imagine. Leaping off again, straight after arriving.'

'Yeah, you're right,' he sighed, 'Parting will be such sweet sorrow, Belle.'

'Oh, what a beautiful thing to say,' she replied, admiringly. 'It's like something a poet would say, or a songwriter.'

'Yeah, or like William Shakespeare would come out with,' coughed Pacer. If that don't make an impression, nothing will, he thought.

When they finished breakfast, Quincy collected their plates, telling Pacer that one of the guest rooms was now vacant if he cared to take a shower there and spruce himself up. His offer was taken up and Pacer returned, fresh-faced and bushy tailed, having shaved and changed his tee-shirt, white as his crowned teeth.

'I'll be on my way then,' he said, approaching Belle, holding her close. 'I'm gonna miss you,' he breathed, kissing her ear.

'Me, too,' she soothed, brushing back her sun-kissed hair from her neck, reaching up and kissing him full on his lips, with Quincy looking on. 'Hey, you two. Are you sure you're lookin' to go your separate ways? You can stay here, get you workin' with the band tonight.'

'If only,' sighed Pacer, gazing into Belle's eyes, before surrendering their embrace.

The big-hearted bar owner could see they were suffering, even though it hadn't been 24 hours since they first set eyes on each other. He didn't see any sense in them prolonging it. He walked to where the Cadillac was parked, opened her rear door, reached in and brought out the singer's guitar in its case.

'I've bin meanin' to ask you about this here geetar,' he declared. 'I'd like to take a look, see what taste you got, used to own a Fender Telecaster back in the day when I was young and much slimmer than now,' he chuckled.

Pacer opened the case and handed his guitar over. 'It's the same model that Elvis used. A Gibson J-200. It was my father's,' he smiled.

Quincy handed back the guitar. 'Aw, before you go you gotta play and sing something for me, in return for providing you with that breakfast you jest ate!' he demanded cheerfully.

'Sure,' said Pacer, slinging the acoustic instrument over his shoulder, re-tuning it, producing a plectrum and strumming a few chords. 'Let's see, now,' clearing his throat and gazing tenderly at Belle. 'One for the road, you might say. Paul Simon's 'Graceland'.'

Pacer had chosen that particular song, hoping that the lyrics would stretch Belle's imagination enough to get her thinking about joining him on the rest of his crusade to Graceland.

The impression they made on the girl from New York City tantalised her imagination, stretched by Pacer's subtle choice of music. The sadness of farewell lingering on her face evaporated. She sang with him every time the chorus came round...

Those moments back in Henderson's 'departure lounge', far away in the UK, were a million miles from happiness. Laying back on stacked pillows amid medical apparatus to keep him breathing, his receding white hair almost matched the whiteness on the satin pillows.

His nurse, Tanya, was with him, as was his dog, Rex, stretched out at the foot of the bed, asleep. The dying man was too weak to grasp the phone she was now holding near his mouth after dialling the singer's number.

Outside the bar room, Pacer and Belle were harmonising Graceland's chorus together, with Quincy clapping along. Suddenly the singalong was interrupted by the phone ringing.

Pacer quickly slung off his guitar aware that only one person would be calling. Grabbing his phone from his jeans pocket, flashbacks of the thief damaging the locking mechanism on the trunk, he felt a pang of guilt.

'Hello', he ventured. 'Mr Henderson?'

'Yes,' came the feeble reply. 'How far? ... how far?'

'How far?' asked Pacer, disturbed by his failing voice, its vagueness. He repeated what he'd explained the day before: 'Covered 500 miles yesterday, slept overnight in the Cadillac, as you wanted, and now I'm hitting the road again, hoping to do another 500.'

There was a long pause... 'Just be sure you do that. I'm countin' on you to do that.'

Henderson's breathing sounded deathly laboured.

'I promise you, Mr Henderson, if I don't make it by tomorrow or the following day, the anniversary, you can keep what you offered me. That's why I'm gonna make it. Fleetwood and me.' Pacer's voice sounded steeped in emotion. He envisaged making it to Graceland, but what about Willard Henderson...?

Seven

TROUBLE

The phone call had poured cold water on 'Graceland'. Washed away, like a bad mood. His head bowed deep in thought, Pacer picked up his guitar and placed it in its case. Meanwhile his companions stood silent... waiting.

Facing them, not mentioning the phone call, he sighed. 'Maybe we'll get together one day, finish the song without any sad interruptions.'

He shook Quincy's hand, thanking him for his hospitality, thoughtlessly tossing the guitar into the back of the Cadillac, showing no concern when it landed on his Stetson crushing it out of shape.

'C'mon, Belle, I'll drop you off on my way. That is,' he intoned, 'unless you.'

There was no reply. Instead, she hugged Quincy and sat in the passenger seat, staring straight ahead as though indifferent to Pacer's sad demeanour.

During the short distance to her relatives' home, not a word was spoken until Belle got out of the Fleetwood. 'Stay here,' she said. 'I'll go write down my address and mobile number for you. I won't be long.'

'Won't be long,' mumbled Pacer, having been waiting for over five minutes, during which time his mind was on one thing, getting to Memphis before Henderson died.

'Where the hell is she,' he groaned, in two minds whether to make a break for it, thinking she wouldn't turn up at all, noticing how empty she seemed.

He was waiting with the engine running, outside one of several up-market residencies dotted along a tree-lined avenue. He was about to hit the car's horn to get her attention when Belle appeared, scampering down the driveway carrying a holdall. Slinging it across the rear seat, she flopped down next to Pacer, breathless.

'Thought you were only going to write down your address and email for me. Couldn't find a pen, Belle?' he quipped.

'I got kinda held up,' she replied, pointing at the holdall.

'Where do you want me to take that?' he shrugged, not looking too pleased. 'I gotta get going, you know. Henderson's on his way out and...'

Belle turned in the seat. 'Go then,' she interrupted, 'and turn on the air-conditioning if you've any sympathy for me. It's hot as hell in here. My god, it was hard work telling my aunt and uncle.'

'Telling them what?' he insisted, driving away.

'That these cheese and ham rolls I've just knocked up are for you and me.'

Taking his eyes of the road, glancing at her. 'But we've only just had breakfast, Belle.'

'Don't you get it?' she groaned, 'Wake up, Pacer. I'm going with you to Graceland.'

He gave a whoop, with a blast on the horn.

'Meanwhile,' she added, 'when we get to eat those rolls, you can eat the poor little pig. I'll enjoy the cheese.'

Back on the highway, Pacer's mood had lifted considerably, knowing he was going to have Belle's company for the rest of the journey. Not once, in the 24 hours since they first set eyes on each other at the service station had she given any hint on being keen on going to Memphis with him, though he'd tried his best, wooing her with Paul Simon's profound lyrics. Her apparent indifference, the silent treatment on their way back to her relatives, seemed to confirm it.

Pacer was curious to know why she suddenly had a change of heart. 'You know something...' he remarked.

'What?' she asked, gazing into the car's vanity mirror checking her appearance.

'You had me thinking, back there, seeing you entering that house, it would be for the last time, seeing the silent mood you were in.'

Belle turned, looking puzzled. 'I wasn't being moody,' she replied. 'I had a lot of thinking to do, whether or not to be here with you and if so, worrying about how my aunt and uncle would react, mean enough to contact my parents. If that's what you call being moody,' she pouted. 'Well, I call it concentrated, practical thinking. I explained to them that we weren't heading to Las Vegas to get hitched, but delivering one pink Cadillac to Graceland. They were so thrilled by the story, I felt they wanted to come along.'

She leaned across the bench seat and planted a kiss on his cheek. 'Satisfied, now?'

'You explained that beautifully, Belle.' he smiled. 'The thing is, you took so long to come back out of that house I thought it was all over, almost before it had begun.'

'Funny thing is,' she laughed, closing the vanity mirror, 'That Graceland song really got me wishing I could go there right then but that phone call from the old man spoilt the moment. You ended the call and just stood there not saying a word. Me and Quincy didn't know what to say, seeing the look on your face. I presumed it was about Mr Henderson, but Quincy wouldn't have known anything, other than your pilgrimage to Graceland. So do you want to tell me? Or is it too tough a question, knowing how you feel about that sick old man?'

'He sounded even worse than he did yesterday,' Pacer sighed. 'I'm worried I'm not going to make it in time to wire through proof to him, seeing the Cadillac outside Graceland, or near enough. It's his dying wish, Belle.' His frustration was evident. 'I cannot let him down. I'm dreading the next call won't be from him, but his nurse.'

What a difference a day made. Henderson's rapid deterioration meant that Pacer's mission to hand over the Cadillac to Graceland's assignees was now a desperate race against time. They had left Quincy's Bar at 8.30am, with 600 miles ahead of them. Pacer figured, that all being well, with no hold-ups, they could travel 400 plus miles that day, only stopping to refuel and give the car a rest while they had a coffee break. The cheese and ham rolls would keep them going until the end of the day and there was bottled water on board.

With all that in mind, the road ahead almost clear of traffic, Belle sidled up, placed her head on his shoulder, heartening the pleasantries of getting to know more about each other. There was chemistry between them. The only time they stopped talking was when they had to separate at the service station rest rooms.

With Henderson almost at death's door, keeping to the rule of not exceeding 50mph, Pacer rationalised that rules were only made to be broken, otherwise what was the point of having them in the first place? They were making good time, having covered 300 miles, but cruising at such low speed, hour after hour, was getting under Pacer's skin. The Cadillac hadn't missed a beat since leaving New York, which hadn't gone unnoticed by her driver. Meanwhile, Henderson's heart was due to miss more than just a beat at any given moment, which also hadn't gone unnoticed. Pacer's cowboy boot put pressure on the throttle, slowly raising the speed, from 50 to 60, keeping it there for the next 30 miles, then raising it to 65. Belle was asleep, still resting on his shoulder. Pacer's knowledge of car engines certified his belief that all was well with the old girl. Not even a whimper from her. That was, until the thermostat dial indicated that the V8 engine was overheating.

Pulling into the side of the highway and stopping, it woke Belle. 'Why have we stopped here on the highway?' she yawned, raising her head.

'She's overheating,' groaned Pacer. 'I forgot to check the radiator for water when we stopped for gas. I've been pushing her a bit, raising her speed. I think she'll be okay when she cools down. I'll top her up with the can in the trunk. Wait for her to stop spitting, first though.'

Sure enough, soon they were back on the road again. This time, the cowboy boot behaved itself. Pacer knew when to ease up. If the engine blew its gasket, the game would be up. Willard Henderson wouldn't see his dying wish come true and it would mean the contract would be worthless.

They hadn't travelled more than fifteen miles when again, they were forced to stop, filling the radiator with most of the water left in the can. This time, Pacer checked underneath the radiator and saw that it was leaking onto the floor. Putting his foot down, he had put his foot in it. He cursed himself for being so disrespectful to the old girl. They were miles away from any service station but there was no alternative than to try and reach the next one, using their bottled water as a last resort. One thing was sure, the leak would get worse. Disaster could be around the next curve on the road.

The Cadillac was now limping along at 30mph, much to the annoyance of other drivers. In the distance a sign displaying the exit from the highway gave a thread of hope. They were in an area where there were other signs of hope, too. Cattle grazing in fields, rather than miles and miles of uninhabited land.

Running parallel to the highway, a river snaked its way in the same direction, giving hope upon hope of making it to the next service station, plugging the radiator, seeing them to their destination.

Leaving the highway, driving along a deserted road, smoke was drifting from a building near the river's bank and as they drew closer could see that it was derelict, destroyed by a fire. Half the roof was missing, and smoke was rising from an external chimney breast, one side of it, the wall almost demolished.

Parked close to the building, a grey, worse-for-wear motorhome. In its prime, about 25 years ago, the Dodge Ram, 250 RV Roadtrek, would have turned heads, but now, for all the wrong reasons. Beat-up would have been paying a compliment. The massive 4x4 would have had no problem leaving the nearby road, tackling the rough ground leading to the structure, not so for the Cadillac.

Leaving her on the side of the road, Pacer and Belle walked the short distance towards the riverbank, where they had noticed a man fishing. Of rugged appearance, wearing a baseball cap, he reminded Pacer of the film star, Robert Shaw, the boat owner in the film, Jaws. His lightweight, thin-rimmed glasses and moustache clinched the resemblance. The dissimilarity being the small fish wriggling on the end of his line was no shark.

Seeing Pacer filling the can with water, he threw the tiny fish back into the river and walked towards them. He was wearing an open-necked check shirt and brown corduroy trousers tucked into boots. With a catchy smile, he asked. 'Hi. You in trouble with that snazzy-looking Cadillac over there. Overheating?'

'Yeah,' said Pacer, rising to his feet, container full to the brim. 'She got a leak in her radiator and we've used up all our water. Lucky we came off the highway and found this river. Should have enough water to get to the next service station.'

'Oh, sorry to hear it,' said the middle-aged fisherman, curiously weighing them up. 'Where you two heading from, and where you heading to?' he asked gruffly. 'Driving around in such a valuable looking specimen in such beautiful preservation is likely to attract unwarranted attention, whatever you might think. I'd carry a weapon if I were you, son.'

'Not from where I come from.' replied Pacer.

'He's from England,' interrupted Belle, 'They prefer smooth talking their way out of trouble over there,' she said, rolling her eyes. 'Not shoot their way out, like we do.'

'You got a point there, miss,' said the man. 'I only wish it were true in America. One day, maybe. One day,' he sighed.

Pacer was eager to get going again, apologising for not stopping longer. 'Nice meeting you, but we're in a hurry, we're heading for Graceland. C'mon, Belle.'

'Hey, wait a second,' said the friendly stranger. 'I got some radiator sealant somewhere in my Roadtrek, back there. It'll get you to Memphis, I guarantee it. You can call me Cassidy, by the way.'

As the three of them made their way from the riverbank up an incline towards the building, it was noticeable that the angler, lagging behind the others, had quite a limp. The sun was now drifting towards the horizon and the cooler air was to his advantage.

Cassidy was about to enter the Roadtrek, when suddenly, a man appeared in the doorway of the derelict house, holding a small dog in his arms, a yappy little thing, snapping at the two visitors. Its scruffy-looking owner appeared to be Mexican. He was dressed like a Charro, a traditional horseman, wearing decorated parrow pants and short jacket covering a vest. In its day, the brown outfit would have looked really eye-catching, but the plump, greasy-looking character must have worn it for about a lifetime without once having it cleaned. The only thing holding the frayed material together were stains. The man was a hobo and the dog was a Chihuahua. A big, hulking name for such a tiny dog.

'Hey,' he grizzled, chewing on a cheroot. 'Why you no introduce me to your amigos? They have nice Cadillac. I buy eet, make me talk of thee town, si?'

'No,' replied Cassidy, turning to face him. 'You're talked about in town enough already. Take a bath, Sancho.'

'Arrgh, no way, amigo,' he protested. 'Why you not know? Only dirty people use bath. Sancho, he wash in river with thee feessh. Smell like thee rosebush, si?'

Cassidy entered his abode on wheels, leaving the couple chatting to the hobo who invited them into his 'casa de villa', not taking no for an answer. When Cassidy reappeared, he persuaded the youngsters to take up Sancho's inoffensive invitation while he fixed the radiator with sealant. It wouldn't take long and they could be on their way much faster than refusing to look inside Sancho's crumbling bricks and mortar.

Sancho ushered them through the main entrance of the shack, its charred door hanging off its hinges. They were taken aback by what met their eyes. The scene resembled the hideout of a kleptomaniac. It just so happened to be true. Anything the old Mexican had collected that had little use was scattered around the room. The rest of his uncontrollable thefts worth anything were stacked near a fireplace, where a frying pan sizzled and spat fat, cooking a brace of river trout. Part of the retaining wall, left of the chimney breast, had collapsed but with one saving grace: the opening offered a panoramic view of the meandering river, and beyond it, an exquisite vermilion sundown. The living conditions in the fire-swept room spelled destitution. The mixture of unsavoury smells permeating the air would have had Fagin screwing up his nose at such whiffaromas. It was fortunate that there was a strong smell of gutted fish entrails smouldering on the ground, near the fireplace, masking the hobo's body odour.

There was a dilapidated easy chair near the fire upon which the highly-strung Chihuahua had leapt as soon as they entered the room. Sancho swept the dog away with his grubby hand and sat down, tending his fry-up. On the mantelpiece, a framed picture of a Mexican cowboy wearing a large sombrero, riding a grey horse in a rodeo. Pacer gazed at it.

The hobo looked up, pointing his spatula at the image. 'You no recognise me, si?' he smiled, rubbing his unshaven chin with the back of his hand.

'Is that really you?' said Pacer, handling the picture, trying to discern any resemblance, before showing it to Belle.

'Si,' Sancho replied, proudly. 'I was number one rodeo charro in Mexico. Thee best. I ween many prize weeth lariat, or what American cowboy call lasso,' he asserted. Then I break thee back,' he sighed, turning over the fillets. 'I die inside. No more rodeo, no more Sancho. No more horse.' He nodded towards a rusty bicycle leaning against some of the clutter in a corner of the room. A wooden, two-wheeled cart had been welded onto the rear forks, purpose-built to carry his belongings. 'Thee way I ride to thee town. I call him El Caballo, The Horse.'

This once proud, dignified charro, having fallen on the hardest of times, was now a sad, world-weary hobo and compulsive pilferer. The realisation saddened his visitors. They wished that Cassidy would soon arrive.

Changing the subject, Pacer asked Sancho how long he

had lived in the shack.

'Let me see,' he replied, counting on his fingers. 'One...two...three...four, and two more year, I theenk. Thees only place where roof not let in thee rain.'

'What about your friend Cassidy?' asked Belle. 'He doesn't look the staying kind, with that Dodge motorhome. By the way,' she nosed, 'How did he get his limp?'

'He come and go,' said Sancho. 'He travel from county to county. He good weeth thee hands, he call heeself odd job man. Gardener, paint fences, mow thee lawn, cut down trees, he try every theeng. He break leg, fall from tree. He strong man, he steel work hard. I call heem Cassidy. Why?' he confided, spitting into the fire. 'Because he not like me to call heem Hopalong because he limp.' Removing the frying pan from the flames, he continued. 'Hopalong Cassidy was famous American feelm star cowboy. But he like me call heem Cassidy.'

The Chihuahua suddenly started barking like a demented dog, indicating that someone was entering the shack. Seeing Cassidy enter the room, the dog barked even louder.

Sancho covered his ears with his hands, complaining. 'Eh, Conchita, you bark too loud for such a leetle dog. You not leesten. Only make noise when someone try to steal sometheen from Sancho, eh?'

Thankfully, the pooch got the message, but not before Sancho threatened her with his greasy spatula. She darted behind his chair, tail between her legs. 'Wise dog,' he grunted, spitting again into the fire, just missing the fish-laden frying pan.

Handing the car keys over to Pacer, Cassidy said. 'All done. I knew I had some of that sealant somewhere tucked away. Lucky for you,' he added, wryly. 'You never know when you're gonna need it. I left her running for a while. The stuff works better once the engine's warmed up. You'll have no more trouble getting her to where you're heading. Graceland, you say?'

'Yeah,' said Belle, before Pacer had a chance to reply. 'It's Elvis's 45th anniversary since...'

'I know what you're gonna say,' interrupted the handyman, smiling. '45 years since he died, back in '77. You two are gonna join the thousands of his other fans on the sixteenth, the day after tomorrow, right? Which one of you owns the guitar laid out on the back seat? It looks expensive, judging by the quality of the snakeskin-covered case, even though it's not genuine snake.'

'Oh, I've had it a long time,' came the enthusiastic reply. 'It was my father's. I don't know what he paid for it, but I know it's worth a lot of money. It's a Gibson acoustic...'

'Pacer's an Elvis tribute act from England, Mr Cassidy,' gushed Belle, proudly, giving the impression that she had known the performer far longer than just a couple of days.

The conversation was cut short when the Chihuahua appeared from her refuge behind the chair, barking like crazy, heading for the outside. Her erratic behaviour warned her master that he should investigate. The dog was on to something out there.

'I theenk there maybe somtheen Conchita no liked. Maybe somtheen Sancho no like. She smell rat, I theenk, from thee riverbank.'

His opinion hadn't impressed Belle. Looking distressed, it was her turn to seek refuge behind the grubby armchair. The hobo stood swearing at Conchita in Spanish. But once outside, he exploded into English. Two leatherclad bikers had smashed the window of the Cadillac. One of them could be seen hopping onto the pillion of a Harley Davidson, gripping the guitar in its case as they roared away into the last fingers of sunset, in the direction of town some miles along the road. By the time Pacer and the rest had reached the doorway, they only managed a glimpse of the thieves speeding into the distance.

Pacer's face was creased with dismay, seeing his beloved guitar being stolen. He rushed over the rough ground, descended on the Fleetwood and examined the damage. Having already lost his guitar, it was little wonder he felt he was being kicked, already beaten to the ground.

The gathering stood in silence. Sancho was the first to speak, his barking dog tucked under his arm. 'Thee theeving bastards,' he spat. 'I see who they are. You see them, too, Cassidy?'

'Yeah,' he replied, sad eyed, 'Even though I didn't catch their faces, I know where they hang out in the town. The pillion rider was female, the driver had connections. Maybe his girlfriend?'

'Amigo, I theenk I know, also,' declared the wizened Hispanic, oblivious to the Chihuahua struggling to get free of him. 'She have bad name in thee neighbourhood. She steal from her abuela, her own grandmother. There are good bikers and bad bikers. The good, they proud of their machines. They poleesh them, si. But thee bad. Arrgh,' he snorted. 'They weesh to steal. Even from another biker, if they get thee chance.'

'You're right,' asserted Cassidy, before rebuking the old rascal. 'But such a statement coming from you, compulsive, addicted, kleptomaniac, who should be seeing a psychiatrist, is a bit much, I reckon.'

Eight

SURRENDER

There's a superstitious saying: 'Things happen in threes, whether they be good or bad.' Well, three bad things had already pursued the Cadillac during the race to get to Graceland before Henderson died. He had been adamant that the Fleetwood should reach there without so much as a scratch. Chasing the dream of driving along Elvis Presley Boulevard, arriving at the iconic gates, sending a satisfying image of the Fleetwood's condition to Henderson was no longer on the cards. Imagine having to establish a thorough spot-check for any damage. Even if Henderson was too weak to do so himself, there would be someone close by to do his bidding. The dent the suicidal rabbit had inflicted on the bumper was superficial and wouldn't be noticed. Sadly for Pacer, it couldn't be said about the trunk and smashed window.

Dusk had now settled on the sad scene, with nothing else but goodbyes. Pacer felt so gutted about losing his father's guitar, couldn't help being tearful about it. Cassidy and Belle tried to console him, but the loss had hit him hard.

Before driving away, Pacer and Cassidy exchanged mobile numbers, it being a slim chance that the recovery of the guitar was a possibility if luck played a part. Standing in the road after waving them goodbye, the men watched the tail lights of the Cadillac growing dimmer, disappearing into the distance. They had only known the young couple for a very short while but truly sympathised with their run of misfortune. The leaking radiator, the smashed window and above all, the theft of the valuable instrument.

'Hey, I sure feel sorry for those two kids,' sighed Cassidy. 'How much did he say that guitar is worth Sancho? Didn't he say about 2,000 dollars?'

'Si, amigo,' Sancho agreed, covering the rough ground back to their respective dwellings. 'They weel think it much less money paid. Maybe they sell eet for peanuts. Maybe they try sell eet to Sancho,' he grunted. 'Thee bikers veesit me sometimes, they look for stealing, they go away weeth notheen,' he sneered. 'Only want money, but I hide eet. I tell them I have shotgun, like you have, but they come back again. They like vulture, scavenge like thee peeg.'

Cassidy glanced at his watch. Darkness prevailed. He had plans for later that evening, but there was time to invite Sancho in and share a bottle of wine. He told the hobo he would be going into town, his shotgun for backup. He knew where the bikers hung out at night, a rundown bar located on the corner of a busy intersection.

'Now, leesten, John Wayne,' said his concerned house guest, pointing a finger at the shotgun resting in Cassidy's arm, sat at a small table in the cramped space. 'I see you try shoot thee rabbeet weeth that theeng,' he groaned. 'They seet up on back legs, they laugh in thee face at you.'

Cassidy gave a wry smile, adjusting his thin-rimmed glasses before gazing down the barrel. 'You know darned well old friend, I shoot rabbits for a living whenever I got no work. That's why I get plenty of practice.'

'Okay, so I joke, amigo. But I no joke now. Take advice of old Mexican charro. Leave evil bikers alone. Thee geetar, eet is gone. You see no more. Why you care? Not stolen from you.'

Cassidy laid the gun down and fiddled with his wine glass.

'Sancho,' he breathed. 'When I saw the look on that kid's face, white as a sheet, losing that guitar, it killed me inside. I can't explain it ... I really felt his loss.'

The hobo grimaced. 'Ha, as you growing older, Cassidy, weeth thee grey hair begin to show, you growing soft inside. Leesten, amigo, eet not thee only guitar in thee world; why you so sad?'

Cassidy didn't reply. Instead, rising to his feet, he handed Sancho the half-finished bottle of wine. 'Here, take this with my compliments. I'm taking a shower before I get into wearing something suitable for where I'm heading. That bar where the bikers hang out. Someone will be high or drunk enough to be bringing the subject up if I hang around long enough. Stealing will be the main topic of interest there.'

As Sancho headed for his own place, swigging from the bottle of wine, he heard Cassidy's voice calling out. 'If you don't hear me returning tonight, you'll know I've got hold of the guitar, chasing after the Cadillac!'

Sancho turned around and exclaimed. 'Amigo! Leesten! If I no hear you come back thees night, I theenk you dead. Like you stupid brain!'

Cassidy, being true to his word, saying he intended wearing the type of gear that wouldn't look out of place in the circumstances, hadn't held back, looking quite the slick dude, entering the bikers bar. Gone were the shabby fishing clothes, especially the brown corduroy trousers tucked into his boots and baseball cap stabbed with fishing hooks.

In place, a snazzy-looking Mexican bandana wrapped around the head, black leather jacket, tee-shirt and slim black trousers, enough to blend in with the others scattered around the room, dressed like Marlon Brando in "On the Waterfront", white tee-shirts and inevitable bandanas.

Cassidy had parked his Roadtrek out of sight around a

corner. A row of Harley Davidsons leaning on their footrests were lined up outside the bar.

Once inside, Cassidy felt like he had been transported onto the set of a movie, a scene from a 1960s retro bar-room where Hells Angels Motorcycle Club members hung out. A jukebox was blasting 'Angels Never Die'. Central to the room a pool table was in action. The players stopped when they saw the stranger standing near the doorway, taking in the scene. Around 20 bikers were either sat at tables, standing in groups or gathered at the bar close to the jukebox. The walls were awash with pictures of movie stars from another era, mainly the sixties. James Dean and Marilyn Monroe on a Harley motorcycle poster; Marlon Brando and the gang from "The Wild One"; another of James Dean astride his Triumph; and the famous one of Steve McQueen clearing a fence in "The Great Escape", a poster that Cassidy looked particularly interested in, adjusting his glasses as he strode over to study the iconic image in more detail.

A few moments later, a gruff voice behind him asked. 'You know the story behind that poster, mister?'

Already feeling on edge, Cassidy swung round, looking up at the huge, bearded biker towering over him, momentarily lost for words.

'McQueen refused to ride a BMW in the film. He loved British bikes, like James Dean, so riding a German machine would be a betrayal. For this reason, he opted to go with the 1961 Triumph TR6 Trophy that was disguised to resemble German WW2 BMW RT5s, helped with a few alterations and a coat of paint.'

'You don't say,' replied Cassidy. 'Whatever next? You certainly know the secret world of bikes'.

The man mountain grunted his approval, turned and headed for the bar, leaving Cassidy wondering how much paint the biker would have used if ever he decided to repaint his own machine.

Making his way through the room, listening and watching for any signs that gave a clue that the guitar might be in the vicinity, he noticed quite a bit of activity in a corner, near the bar.

Drawing closer, the distinctive aroma of marijuana permeated the air. The banned substance reminded him of his Mexican neighbour's casual indulgence in the pungent herb, when a gentle breeze carried the trace from shack to motorhome.

Cassidy guessed there was either an interesting card game in progress, or something far more relevant that could be music to his ears, like the sound of an acoustic guitar, even though the haunting 'Angels Never Die' was being played on a loop, courtesy of a gaunt, solemn-looking uneasy rider.

Joining the small clique, Cassidy gave a sigh of relief. The sight and sound of a guitar being tortured by a greasy-looking biker seated on a sofa next to an unappealing broad, the snakeskin design guitar case close by, manifested a cold, silent rage.

The couple – Claude and his bird – looked in their late twenties. The pair were well met, similarly attired, shifty-looking and in need of a good scrub, something that any decent biker would have heartily agreed with, even though no such biker existed in the place.

'Stop messing about and play something,' quipped one of the clan, fed up of watching Claude fumble with the strings of the Gibson, having no idea, just yanking at them before letting them twang. 'Or are you just waiting for 'Angels Never Die' to finish on the jukebox?'

Claude's girlfriend butted in, obviously frustrated by such banter. 'Take no notice, honey,' she pouted, wrapping her arm around his shoulder, 'He's just jealous because you're holding it instead of him gettin' to steal it,' she sniped. 'Let's see you playin' it bird brain. Or anyone else of you lookin' on. Claude won't play it 'cos he's a shy person, that's all. All you lookin' on, hopin' he play like AC/DC. He ain't had enough practise yet, that's all, ain't you honey?'

Seeing the two thieves for the first time made Cassidy think even more he had walked onto a film set. Claude's girlfriend resembled Anjelica Huston, Morticia in "The Addams Family". Long black hair, pasty complexion, heavy mascara and blood-red lipstick. Both were dressed head to foot in black. She, wearing a leather jacket over a tee-shirt emblazoned with a skull, tight shorts, knee-high leather boots, net stockings, gothic jewellery and tattoos.

Claude reminded Cassidy of Tommy Lee, Mötley Crüe's drummer, ex-husband of Pamela Anderson. Black hair, goatee beard, studded waistcoat, vest, studded dog collar, sunglasses on forehead, loads of tattoos and jewellery. Unlike the film stars they resembled, they were dishevelled, sleazy and bombed on weed.

Claude was getting tired of his girlfriend sticking up for him. Making excuses, being a bit shy playing the guitar, still learning and so on, knowing full well he'd never even handled a guitar, let alone played one before stealing it. Short on patience, he had now lost interest in having anything more to do with the instrument, other than selling it on. As he laid it down, Cassidy seized an opportunity.

'Hey, buddy, if I gave up on learning the guitar, like you just done, I'd never gotten into a band.'

Claude wasn't in the mood for advice, especially from a stranger. Looking up, he sneered, 'For a start, who said I ever wanted be in a band? And if I don't want to learn how to play the shit thing, it's none of your business.'

'That's right, Claude, you tell 'im,' said his woman chipping in. 'If he's so interested in the geetar, let him take a look, maybe he'll make an offer for it.' While Claude was thinking it over, she quizzed the stranger. 'You a biker, mister? Ain't seen your face in here before,' she flashed.

Cassidy was ready with an answer, half expecting such a query. 'I was passing through town, on my way to see an old biker friend of mine. We gave up riding some years ago, but we still keep in touch. Seeing those Harleys lined up outside got me feeling kinda sentimental, know what I mean? Once a biker always a biker. I had a hankering for a beer so in I came. Still ain't ordered my beer though.'

Claude butted in, having made up his mind about the guitar. He handed it over. 'Check it out, tell me what you think it's worth, being a professional player. Make me an offer for it and I might order that beer you're thirstin' for.'

Luck appeared to be falling into Cassidy's lap, or rather, hands. Strumming a few chords, he stopped. 'Well, for a start, it don't mean a thing if the strings don't zing, and these old strings have just about had it.' He then investigated the maple neck gazing down its length with one eye closed. 'I'm afraid the neck is kinda warped, bowed, like it's been left out in the rain. It won't be in tune until that's fixed. Huh, if you paid more than 100 dollars for it, you was robbed.'

'What about the case?' asked Claude. 'That's gotta be worth something, there aint a scratch on it. He and his partner looked agitated, thinking the stranger might be purposely exaggerating, undermining its true value.

'Well, let's see now,' said the man with no name, thoughtfully scratching his chin. 'Yeah, I think the case could be included in the transaction. By the way, out of curiosity, how much did you pay out, altogether ?'

Claude was too stoned to come up with an immediate plausible answer, too slow. His collaborator stepped in. '500 dollars,' she brazenly asserted, glaring at the biker. 'Claude wouldn't listen to me when I told him he was being conned.'

'You got yourself done, sorry to say. I'm willing to pay 200 dollars for the guitar and 100 dollars for the case. I'll have to get that warped neck fixed and re-string the damn thing, and that won't come cheap.'

Nudging her man in the ribs. 'Take it, Claude. Take the gentleman's money, and let it be a lesson to you next time you get the urge for playin' somethin' you can't play.'

At a snail's pace, Claude obeyed her instructions, languidly placing the guitar in its case, and asking for the 300 dollars before handing it over.

'I'm sorry,' said Cassidy. 'I don't happen to carry that kind of money on me. It's back in my vehicle, around the corner, about 100 yards down the street.'

'Okay, let's go,' said the biker, raised from his stupor by the smell of money. Following behind, his girlfriend whispered, 'Don't go alone ... just in case.'

'No way, honey. This guy is older than me, wearin' glasses, carrying a limp, in need of a wheelchair. He ain't gonna be a problem.'

Arriving at the motorhome, Cassidy invited Claude inside, saying, 'Welcome to my humble abode, no need to wipe your feet.' Smiling broadly, he couldn't have been more friendly.

'Roadtrek, ain't it,' remarked Claude, entering, taking in the expanse on four wheels. 'I had a hankering on owning one of these for gettin' around, but then I settled on a '92 Hummer truck, having what I need for my desires.'

'What kind of purpose might that be?' asked Cassidy, thinking he might reply with some off-the-cuff remark about law-breaking, being so stoned.

'Never you mind,' Claude blurted. 'Let's just say it scares the shit out of some fat-cat driver when I pull them over and ask to lend me some dollar. Know what I mean?'

'Yeah, I sure do,' came the cold answer. 'Lay that case on the bed, down that end there, while I get your money.'

Laying the guitar on the bed, Claude took a pull on his spliff. Turning, he found himself looking down the barrel of pump-action shotgun almost nudging his hook-shaped nose. Gobsmacked, his jaw dropped, likewise the spliff from his mouth.

'That's very clumsy of you, Claude,' groaned Cassidy, stamping on it. 'Not only did you steal that guitar, you try setting fire to my home. What are we gonna do with you?' he derided. 'Well, let's see you taking off those mournful-looking clothes, leaving your underpants and fancy jewellery on, so you still look respectable.'

Claude looked paler than his gothic girlfriend's pasty face. 'You're makin' a mistake, man,' he wailed. 'I'm not gay, I got a girlfriend back there.'

Raising his voice and looking meaner than a contract killer, Cassidy snarled, 'Shut your thieving mouth, and take 'em off like said. I don't intend violating you, boy, just make a mockery of you when you hit the sidewalk out there, for stealing that guitar from my friend, who's come all the way from England with that Cadillac you broke into, to a special anniversary he's attending.'

Standing there, naked, but for his underwear, fear in his eyes, staring down the gun-barrel, it would have been a safe bet that Claude would have retracted the last words uttered to his girlfriend on leaving the bar, 'He ain't gonna be a problem.'

Cassidy poked him in the back with the shotgun, heading for the door, 'You're gonna walk out onto the street and just be grateful you're still wearing something left to hide. Now, open the door and vamoose back to your biker buddies. If you dare!'

Giving him a meaningful push, Claude fell through the

doorway landing flat on the sidewalk amidst the hustle and bustle of night traffic and street life. Not a pleasant position for anyone, even for a lousy, stoned thief.

Cassidy quickly drove away from the astonishing scene, before it got some unwanted attention nosing in wearing a cop uniform. Passing the biker bar he slowed down and threw Claude's clothes through the Dodge's open window, landing near the row of Harleys. He pictured what the bikers would make of it: one of their own, shrinkingly appearing, clutching his garments to his chest, almost in tears.

Speeding out of town, the guitar safe in his possession, Cassidy got on the phone to Pacer, telling him all what had happened, asking him about his whereabouts, and learning that they had stopped for the night at a service station after travelling for almost a couple of hours, feeling dead beat.

Finding out where they were located, Cassidy advised them to get some sleep, that he'd park up near to the Cadillac and wake them early in the morning, knocking on the Cadillac's window and handing over the guitar. Ending the call, he happened to be passing Sancho's shack and toot-tooted as he drove past, signalling to the hobo that all was well, that he wasn't dead as the Mexican predicted he would be, courtesy of the bikers.

Pacer had pulled into the service station 60 miles further down the highway. After filling up with gas he parked as close as he could to the restaurant and adjoining rest-rooms, not wanting to leave the car with its shattered window tempting more trouble. It was around 10.00 pm and Pacer suggested that Belle freshened up at the rest-room first, while he relaxed in the automobile.

Predictably, being female, she had been gone for quite a while, having freshened up, checking her makeup after changing out of her summer dress into more practical clothes: denim jacket and jeans and silky white blouse with a venturesome cleavage. Pacer was about to nod off, when she slid up next to him. Her alluring perfume had the desired effect on the smooth-talking Londoner.

'Mmm, what's the name of that killer perfume?' he breathed, deliberately expressing his curiosity by closing in, almost brushing faces. To his great delight, she suddenly embraced the well-practised seducer and, perhaps not before time, they kissed passionately. Maybe the broken window played a small part inviting balmy night air on a romantic breeze.

Eventually, the singer made another smooth move, this time sliding out of the Cadillac, aware that they would soon have to be sleeping in the rear seat.

With the taste of Pacer's lips still lingering on hers, waiting for his return, purely out of curiosity she opened the glove compartment and discovered some paperwork, including a receipt for the modification work, paid in full to Chess Autos by Elvis Presley. Probing further into its lit depth, her intrusive forefinger triggered the secret compartment to spring open, revealing the Derringer and jewellery Elvis had stowed away, back in '56.

Bewitched, bothered and bewildered, Belle's eyes dazzled almost as much as the jewellery. Lifting the items from the compartment, she laid them on her lap. The cabin's absence of light was enough excuse for her to try the diamond ring on her finger, curl the sparklers around her throat and admire them in the car's vanity mirror, the gems an adornment to the girl's breath-taking natural beauty.

Forcing herself to look away from the mirror, intending to return the items to the compartment, she instinctively looked over her shoulder. There, gazing through the rear, smashed window, an ugly looking character, his grimy hand, about to snatch the necklace from her throat. Instead of screaming for help, she grabbed the Derringer from her lap, leaned over the seat and pointed it.

'Listen, fuckface. This is only a little Derringer,' she bravely informed him, trying to keep her hand from not shaking, 'but large enough to blow a hole through your head,' she gulped. 'Now beat it, before my boyfriend returns.'

Her threat worked. Had Belle been aware the gun wasn't loaded she would have probably screamed. The intruder turned and scampered away like a rabbit with a greyhound on its tail.

A few moments later, Pacer arrived, clutching a pyramid of hot food containers, fresh from the restaurant. He almost dropped the lot, seeing Belle, almost hysterical, holding the Derringer in one hand, the necklace in the other. He placed the meals on the rear seat as Belle got out of the car and threw her arms around his neck, still holding both items.

Sobbing, she told him what had happened while he was gone. 'I looked inside the glove compartment. Maybe I shouldn't have, but I found these in it,' she babbled. Unwrapping her arms, she gave them to him. 'Some guy tried to steal them, but then he ran when I pointed the gun.' Trembling, she eased the ring off her finger. 'This was in there too, all of it was in a kinda secret cubby-hole.'

Pacer looked stunned. 'How the hell did they find their way in there?' he pondered, easing Belle back into her seat, comforting her, before checking out the cavity, wondering if Henderson knew about it and if so, why hadn't he told him it was there. There was only one way to find out, but he would have to wait until morning. It wouldn't have been fair to ask him now, it being around 5.00 am in the UK.

Still feeling upset, Pacer managed to get Belle to eat some of the takeaway. The incident had left them feeling bereft of anything like the passionate desire they'd had for each other earlier. Curled up on the back seat, Pacer's mobile was ringing. It was Cassidy telling them the good news about his beloved guitar, that he was on his way, asking him how far he had travelled and where he could catch up, get some sleep, he'd see them in the morning.

Claude wasn't in a bad mood after been poked out of the motorhome by the barrel of a shotgun, minus his clothes. No: he was raging, looking for vengeance, laughed off the face of the Earth on entering the bar. The only person not joining in on the teasing and giggling was his embarrassed girlfriend as she helped him get dressed.

'I warned you not to go there on your own, Claude,' she scolded, pulling his vest over his head. 'How come he got you takin' all your clothes off?'

'With a pump-action shotgun,' came the withering reply, as he zipped up his pants. 'If I'd had my shooter with me he would have been dead meat. He took that guitar but that wasn't enough for the scumbag, he went and humiliated me, forced me out of his motorhome, makin' me look a fool havin' to run back here like the town's sicko.'

'I seen what looked like a motorhome, close by to where we stole from that pink Cadillac, right next to that old shack where the Mexican hobo been livin', next to the river.'

The aggression on the biker's face turned to intrigue. 'Is that so,' he said, eyes narrowing. 'Yeah, it makes sense. He said he was going to hand the guitar back to its rightful owner. Yes, he might still be there, even if the Cadillac ain't. I don't give a shit about the guitar, It's his ass I want.'

With that, he turned and addressed a number of bikers who had been listening in on their conversation. 'Hear that,' he railed, 'the son of a bitch might be holed up near Sancho's hovel if I ain't mistaken. I'm headin' over there right now, stopping at my place to collect the shooter. Who's comin' with me?' he appealed dramatically, searching their faces. 'If the motorhome is there, we can creep up on him leavin' our bikes far enough back, so he won't be warned.'

Four of the bikers, unable to hide their reluctance, agreed to accompany him anyway, out of bravado.

Claude, now pumped up by their loyalty, took his girlfriend to one side. 'Mistletoe,' he began.

'Shut it, Claude,' she hissed, hoping no-one had heard him. 'I hate being called Mistletoe. I hate my name, Just because I happened to be born on Christmas Day and my mother was a compulsive attention-seeker.'

'Sorry, I was only tryin' to be nice, askin' you to roll a spliff for me.'

'Well, watch it next time, make sure you don't slip up,' she spat. 'I'd preferred you'd had called me Holly, Ivy, anything bar that stupid name.'

'Okay,' surrendered the biker, rolling his eyes, having been preached about it many times before. 'But I ain't promising nothin'.' He drew her close and gave her a hug. 'Now, about that spliff, make it a strong one, I'm gonna need it for nervous tension for where I'm headin'.'

The relaxing sound of Hispanic music being played on a beat-up portable radio could be heard emanating through the cracks, crevices and crumbling masonry of the unsafe structure. Within its walls, the greasy-vested down-and-out, dozed peacefully in his easy chair near the fire's dying embers. His dog on his lap, an old-fashioned oil lamp softly illuminated the spooky encasement. Useless junk strewn over the floor or piled in a comer, the hoard of a kleptomaniac. The Bible Sancho had been reading slowly slipped from his grubby-nailed fingers and fell to the floor. The strains of the acoustic guitar from the radio now competed with the louder strains of snoring, Sancho forever dreaming of being a charro riding a thoroughbred stallion.

With the open Bible resting at his feet, Sancho suddenly awoke, disturbed by the distinct throttle rumblings of a combined force of Harley Davidsons becoming louder as they reached the shack, silenced when their engines cut out.

Sensing danger, the Chihuahua leapt from her master's lap, making a stand near him, ready to protect with her life, for what good it would have accomplished. Barking hysterically, the dog had raised the hobo's wakefulness to the level of being prepared for the worst.

Her keen sense of smell nosed Claude's B.O., something the pooch could be proud of considering she had been asleep on her master's lap all night.

Cautiously leading the way into the god-forsaken abode, theatrically searching with his handgun, like an F.B.I. agent on the trail of a deadly deaf and blind serial killer on the loose. The comical sight of five bikers huddled together, creeping up on the Mexican and his howling dog was priceless. The kleptomaniac's knick-knack storage of junk encased them, along with his rusty bicycle-cum-cart and camp bed getting in their way. By the time they managed to reach Sancho, if he had wished to do so, he could have escaped by way of the collapsed wall once attached to the chimney breast.

Stoned out of his head thanks to Mistletoe's generously filled spliff, Claude pointed his gun at Sancho babbling something at him, but overpowered by the dog snapping at his biker boots, Claude lethargically propelled the courageous mutt flying with his footwear.

Sancho had been taken aback by his uninvited visitors, raiders of the lost motorhome, but now he had a good idea why, having heard Cassidy give that blast on his horn.

Snarling expletives, the biker grabbed the intimidated

vagabond by the vest, yanked him off the chair and shook him. 'Where is he? I wanna kill him!'

'Que?' said Sancho, looking puzzled. 'I no understand, amigo.'

'The guy with the motorhome, pigbrain!'

'Motorhome? no see motorhome, only peenk Cadillac. Eet stop for water for engine. Sancho tell truth. He no lie.'

Claude let him fall back into the chair, aggrieved by the hobo's cover-up. 'Lie, you don't know the meanin' of it,' he growled. 'That son-of-a-bitch stole my guitar, made me feel like some kind of pervert walkin' the streets!'

Sancho realised he had to own up about the motorhome being there, seeing the murderous look on the biker's face. 'Ah, si,' he enthused, tapping his forehead. 'Sancho tired, but he theenk back. He remember now. Motorhome, eet stop for moment. Thee driver say he on way to Mexico. He join thee drugs cartel in Mexico City. Heem, he bad man, he dangerous. He say, 'Geeve me directions to Mexico.' He say he lost hees map. I tell heem, Sancho, he not know the way even to San José. Then he go.'

Claude's impatience exploded with wet gob saliva. 'Take me for a fool! Lyin' through those stinkin,' rottin,' teeth! Look, before I get really sore, where can I find him? Or else that mutt ends up in the river!'

There was no way out of the situation for the Mexican now. Only the truth.

'Okay,' shrugged the crafty old devil. 'But no say I no warn you from heem. He armed weeth shotgun, knife and gun. The hombre, he well armed.'

'I don't give a shit what he's carryin',' spat Claude, pointing his gun at the whimpering Chihuahua trembling under the camp bed. 'Where's he runnin' to? Or else the dog gets it.'

'He see you steel thee guitar from thee Cadillac, steel eet

from hees amigo. You never catch heem, he half thee way to Memphis already. Sancho swear on thee Holy Bible,' pointing to the Book at his feet, open-paged, revealing the Ten Commandments. 'See, I no lie. You never catch heem.'

'Is that so,' sneered Claude, shoving the shooter into his waistband and turning to his faithful followers. 'Reckon our Harleys can catch up with him before he reaches Memphis in that old motorhome?' he asked, proudly.

'You make beeg meestake,' interrupted Sancho smiling confidentially. 'Hees pump-action shotgun, eet very powerful. Shoot beeg hole in Harley. Kaput! You walk home. si?'

Claude, still completely stoned, took a long time weighing up the hobo's words, finally declaring, 'We'll see about that. There's more than one way to catch a rat...'

Nine

ALL SHOOK UP

The old hobo had done his utmost to deter the bikers from going after Cassidy but not owning a phone, there was no way of letting him know he was being chased by a gunman high on vengeance, as well as drugs.

However, Claude had no intention of hitting the highway that night. Instead, they headed back to town and the bar room before getting a few hours sleep. Claude had taken heed of Sancho telling him that their motorbikes, up against the massive Dodge Roadtrek and its well-armed driver, wouldn't be a good idea, and his handgun was no match for a powerful pump-action shotgun.

In the bar room, Claude told his girlfriend his plan. At the break of dawn, he and the bikers would be chasing the motorhome that was chasing the pink Cadillac. Claude's head had begun to clear, enough for him to remember what Cassidy had said while in the motorhome: that he was returning the guitar to someone who was going to a special anniversary in Memphis. 'Where else but Graceland,' he told his girlfriend. 'That's where we'll find that old Roadtrek. How many of those will you see parked up somewhere close to those gates?'

Arriving at the designated service station, Cassidy had no trouble finding where the Cadillac was parked. After filling up with gas, he put his head down for the few hours left before dawn when he would knock on the Cadillac's window and present the guitar to its rightful owner. Pacer would, no doubt, be ever grateful, insisting on filling the Roadtrek's tank with gas, but beaten to it.

6.30am and dawn had settled on the subdued service station. Cassidy had slept well, considering the dramatic events of yesterday. The first thing on his mind, taking the guitar to where the Cadillac stood, not far from the restaurant. For some reason, instead of taking the instrument in its case, he lamely carried it like a washed-up, destitute musician hitching a ride to nowhere.

Peeping through the Cadillac's shattered window, he smiled as he set eyes on the sleeping duo embraced in each others arms despite the growing activity in the car park.

Cassidy slung the guitar over his shoulder, cleared his throat and started singing an Elvis classic, 'Tryin' To Get to You'.

Seeing his croaky rendition had achieved the desired effect, Cassidy cut short his chirping and opened the door. 'C'mon you two lovebirds, untangle yourselves, breakfast is waiting, and I'm starving..!'

Before entering the restaurant, they made their way to the motorhome, wisely leaving the two holdalls and guitar there, considering the Cadillac was in a bit of a state security-wise. On their way back, Pacer commented on the way Cassidy had performed the song. 'That was impressive, you singing that number and playing it.' he enthused. 'Elvis performed 'Tryin' To Get To You' on his Comeback TV Special in '68.'

'Yeah,' said Cassidy. 'I was blown away when Elvis sang 'Tryin' To Get To You'.'

'I've seen that show time and time again.' replied Pacer. 'Elvis, all in black leather. It was the best number he performed in his set.'

'There you go,' chuckled Cassidy, wrapping his arm

round Pacer's shoulder, giving him a warm hug as they entered the restaurant. 'Two minds thinkin' alike..'

Belle, being vegan, ordered cereal and banana pancakes from the pretty waitress. Meanwhile, Pacer and Cassidy went for eggs, bacon, sausages, hash browns, toasted muffin, fruit and coffee.

While waiting for the food, the trio became engrossed in conversation regarding the rescuing of the guitar and how Cassidy had dealt with Claude, brandishing his shotgun to get his message across, teaching him a lesson, making him lose his clothes, and so on. But as the exchange continued, Pacer began to look uneasy.

'Cassidy,' he interrupted. 'I have to ask you. Why have you been doing all this for us? Going out of your way, recovering the guitar, driving through the night, chasing us with it. It just don't seem to add up. Belle and me, we only met you for about ten minutes back there. Don't get me wrong, man.' he groaned, holding up his hands. 'I'm so grateful but it just...' Pacer looked more uneasy than ever, having unwrapped his angst.

Cassidy responded with a low sigh, before lowering his head. Then, folding his arms, he glanced at Belle, before directing his gaze at the singer. 'That's a fact, son, you're right,' he smiled. 'I get it... but I've known you far longer than ten minutes. How old are you? Wait, I'll tell you. 24, right?'

Pacer looked bemused, The fact that he had guessed his age wasn't all that remarkable, but the 'longer than ten minutes' comment was far from being unremarkable and worthy of querying. 'Yeah,' he replied, nodding agreement. 'You guessed right. How about that, Belle? Thanks Cassidy, that's a relief, I always worry I look a lot older!'

There was laughter all round, loud enough for diners to turn heads. Pacer asked what he meant by the strange, ten minutes remark he had made. 'It's kinda bugging me,' he insisted.

Cassidy's response was to haltingly lean back in his seat, wrap his arms behind his head and gaze through the nearby window, his face sullen. The seconds ticked away. 'Are you okay?' said Belle, 'Anything wrong?'

'Huh, you could say that,' Cassidy sighed, turning from the window, dewy-eyed, giving her a sombre smile.

'Pacer,' he said softly, reaching over the table, laying his hand on his shoulder. 'I hope you don't get mad at me, for what I'm gonna say ... but it's been on my mind and rightly so, that I tell you, even though you might not want to hear it. I'm your father.'

The shock on Pacer's face was a hammer blow of disbelief; although Belle believed, what with Cassidy singing his head off, he might have snatched a spliff off Claude before throwing him out. Either way, she braced herself for what was going on in Pacer's mind.

Taking his hand away from the singer's shoulder, Cassidy leaned back in his seat readying himself for what he expected. Fireworks! His only hope, one or two being dampened. After initial astonishment at someone declaring such nonsense, Pacer displayed his sense of humour, spluttering with laughter, pointing his finger at Cassidy. 'You, my father?' he chortled, with a sideways glance at Belle. 'You can't be serious. My father looks nothing like you. I've got photos of him, back home.' Pacer suddenly stopped sniggering, seeing tears welling in Cassidy's eyes. 'C'mon, man,' he sighed, 'I ain't falling for that one. You're going a bit too far now. Let's change the subject, yeah?'

At that precise moment, Pacer's iPhone rang. It was Henderson, checking in on him. 'Excuse me,' he said. 'It's Henderson. Shuush, he thinks I'm travelling alone.

'Hello, Mr Henderson.'

'Why ain't you rung me? You should be there now.' Pacer was surprised how alert the old man seemed, considering he was at death's door the day before.

'We're... I mean, I'm only about three hours away from Memphis. Just stopped for breakfast. Should hit Graceland by mid afternoon. All according to traffic.'

'Hell and confusion!' blasted Henderson. 'Stop saying WE, dammit! Makes me feel nervous. You're takin' more time than a turtle,' he grizzled. 'Any damage, any scratches on that Cadillac? I'll know about it. You hear, boy?' Pacer went pale, cringing.

He tapped the bulge on the inside pocket of his denim jacket. 'Oh, by the way, Mr Henderson,' he piped. 'That gun and jewellery in that secret compartment of the Fleetwood. I don't remember you mentioning it, back at the Manor. Did you know they were there?'

'Gun? Jewellery? what in hell's name are you talkin' about?' he wheezed, causing a bout of coughing. 'Secret compartment in the Cadillac. Where, in God's name?'

'In the glove compartment. I pressed a tiny button and it opened. They were in there. I've kept them on me for safekeeping, after the window...'

Whatever medication Henderson was on must have been upgraded. Either that, or the poor man was experiencing the last throes of survival. 'Huh? After the window? Spit it out, what window?'

'Er. after the rear window slipped down a couple of inches, that's all,' he lied. 'Couldn't take the chance of it slipping any further, just in case. Impossible to keep an eye 100 per cent of the time.'

'Okay, son, fair enough. But put them back where you found them,' he grunted. 'I got a good idea how they got there. Elvis must have placed them when I wasn't lookin'. When he was in that showroom. They belong to Graceland.

See that you do that. I trust you.'

The line went dead, leaving Pacer wondering if Henderson had Holy connections. Like being in line for the Second Coming.

Belle was more perceptive than Pacer, him being in total denial regarding the claim of fatherhood. Seeing how sullen Cassidy remained while he was on the phone, she felt, if he was only joking, why would he keep up the pretence while the singer was distracted?

She was about to challenge Pacer, asking him not to dismiss Cassidy completely, when the breakfasts arrived.

With the arrival of the mouth-watering, distinctive smell of bacon, overpowering the rest on the menu, all thoughts regarding parenthood were now seemingly put on ice. Belle's only distraction, seeing Pacer's piggy rashers being mutilated on his plate before forked into his gluttonous piehole, where mutilation was further masticated and then dispatched into Peppa Pig-like acidic sludge. Given the chance, that's how she would have described the whole filthy process.

As the waitress collected their plates, it was noticeable that Cassidy's appetite had forsaken him. His breakfast, more played about with than eaten. Belle saw an opportunity to question his morbidity further, but was ambushed.

'Hey,' asked Pacer, licking his greasy lips. 'Waste not, want not. I'm hungry enough to order another breakfast. Cassidy, pass your plate over, I'll do the honours for you.'

Cassidy was about to do no such thing, unimpressed by Pacer's hedonistic attitude, deliberately dismissing signs that something was amiss. Casually he produced a photograph from his jacket with one hand, passing his plate over to the waitress with the other, much to the singer's dismay.

'Take a look at this here photo,' he sighed, having controlled much of the emotion he had shown earlier. 'It might whet your appetite more than what's on that plate.'

Belle sat back in her chair, having a fair idea that evidential evidence was about to follow.

Pacer studied the creased photograph. His reaction: 'Hey, that's me,' he smiled, 'when I was about ten.' Staring uneasily at Cassidy, he handed the photo back. 'Who gave you that?' he asked, suspiciously.

Belle had heard enough. Glaring at him, she fired, 'Wake up, Pacer. Wake up and smell the coffee. You asked him why he had reason to put himself in danger with those bikers. Well, it seems like here's your answer,' she declared, nodding at Cassidy.

Pacer was taken aback by her stance, expressing her view with such raw emotion in her, it worked, or maybe the smell of coffee being placed under his nose by the waitress.

Noting Belle's opinion, Cassidy then acknowledged Pacer's question. 'No-one gave me the photo,' he said. 'I was the one who took it. Just before the camera clicked, a dog bit you, remember? The scar is plain to see on the back of your hand.'

Pacer couldn't argue with that.

'I had a fair idea that you were my son,' he continued, 'back at the motorhome, when I saw the snakeskin guitar case on the back seat of the Cadillac. I once owned it. I named you Pacer, from Elvis's character in one of his movies.' He looked Pacer straight in the eyes. 'It was a shock, believe me.' He returned the photo to his jacket pocket. 'Some people might say it was one hell of a coincidence meeting up the way it happened. On the other hand, I prefer to think it was God talking.'

Pacer didn't seem to know what to think, say or do. He sat there tense as a guitar string.

'Before I had time to process it properly, deciding how I was going to tell you, you had hightailed it back on the highway.' Raising his coffee to his lips before placing the cup back on the table, 'I'm sorry,' he said, offering his hand to Pacer. There was no response from his estranged son, only silence. A rebuff.

Disheartened, Cassidy lowered his head. 'All I know,' he sighed, 'it's been one hell of a shock for both of us.' He then looked up. 'More so for you. If I had just happened to turn up on your doorstep, that would have been bad enough,' he frowned, 'but now, 4,500 miles away, out of the blue and in weird circumstances, it's worse on you.'

'Yeah,' interrupted Pacer, stony-faced, deliberately not making eye contact with the man he didn't recognise from his childhood, clean-shaven, no glasses, East London accent. 'It's only harder because you made it that way, fifteen years ago. Right?'

Belle sensed that if they continued on that path, with Pacer becoming more agitated by the minute, there would be little hope of reconciliation between father and son. Interrupting, she implied, because Pacer was so young when it happened, he would have only been told his mother's side of things, that there are always two sides to a story. Both, in fairness, should be listened to. Here was the chance for it to happen, otherwise...

With some coaxing, the young singer gave in.

'Well,' began Cassidy, nervously clearing his throat, 'My head was in a mess, long before your mother and I broke up. I'd lost my job at the saw mills where I was the manager. We were made redundant due to the recession in the UK, and no prospect of re-employment on the horizon. Having never been out of work before, I got badly depressed. You were in school, your mother out working, I ended up spending most of the day in the local pub drowning my sorrows, screwed by my state of mind. Your mother, thinkin' otherwise, having red hair and quite a temper showed me the door, more than one occasion...'

With some persuasion from Belle, the trio had left the restaurant feeling far more destined than when they had entered it. And although Pacer wasn't ripened enough to give his father the stereotype expectant hug seen in movies, he was keen on telling him what the phone call with Henderson was all about, and that reaching Graceland before Henderson passed away was his priority. However, his main concern at that moment, was whether or not the leak in the Cadillac's radiator would remain plugged until they arrived there.

His father, intent on staying by his side for as long as possible, had immediately offered to tag along for the rest of the journey, ensuring that any mishaps that might happen, he would be there to be of assistance. Pacer's steely-blue eyes had lit up at the suggestion, for it would also become a journey of rediscovery for both men.

Before getting into their vehicles, the belated hug was now being shared between the three of them. Pacer had found it too much of a stretch, calling his fellow companion Cassidy, Dad. It felt strange. At least for now.

Hitting the highway again, the Cadillac took the lead, with the hefty Roadtrek following behind. Cassidy wasn't going to chance checking his rear-view mirror and finding the Fleetwood no longer behind him. With any luck, in around three or four hours, keeping their speed to 50 mph. they should be rockin' up on Elvis Presley Boulevard delivering one pink Cadillac containing precious jewellery, near as dammit to the gates of Graceland. There would be no problem parking. Henderson, aware that thousands of fans would be there for the anniversary had paid in advance, online, to park directly opposite, in Graceland's parking lot. All Pacer had to do was use his iPhone for identification at the entrance.

All being well, the decision had been made, once the transaction had been completed, to move on to Nashville for a few days. A chance to unwind and visit a few bars that Cassidy would have been familiar with, places where a good ol' Country band would be kickin' ass. Pacer would soon be returning to London where he would have to explain to his mother about his father, who he had 'bumped into on his travels'. If, at the time, there happens to be a fly on the wall observing her reaction, no doubt, her voice will have created tremendous wing-beating through the nearest open window.

Driving, Pacer was now in a good frame of mind, singing along to Willy Nelson's hit, 'On The Road Again'. True, under the circumstances. However, the radio was too loud for Belle's comfort, judging by the way she had her fingers in her ears.

Pacer had good reason to be singing. Willard Henderson seemed to have made a miraculous recovery, making a U-turn from death's door. He had also made amends with his father following behind. Almost at journeys end, beside him a stunningly beautiful American called Belle. What more could he ask for?

Cruising behind, whistling a happy tune, himself having made amends with his one and only son, Cassidy was also at peace. The road ahead was light with traffic, the sun was beating down and the Roadtrek's powerful V8 engine was running smooth as silk, not missing a beat. What could possibly go wrong, he thought, with the gods looking down on me with such zeal, kindness and compassion.

A lot, by the sound of things.

Bearing down on him from behind, the intimidating raw rumble of a 6.0 V8 350 horsepower engine. 'Oh, no,' wailed Cassidy, seeing the tank-like Hummer truck in his rear-view mirror. 'Bloody Claude!'

The bikers had caught up with him by luck more than judgement. Claude had expected the Roadtrek to be somewhere in the vicinity of Graceland, with the Cadillac in the same area. He would have been overjoyed, seeing the old motorhome lumbering along, perfect for targeting a couple of tyres with the Police Issue, Colt 38 Revolver. When a shot rang out, Cassidy contacted Pacer.

Don't panic!' he yelled down the phone, 'It's not a burst tyre, just a gun being fired! Look out your window, you'll see why! I know this stretch of road, there's an exit up ahead, you just keep on going, Claude is after my blood, not yours! See you in Memphis!'

Claude was certainly bent on vengeance, accompanied by a small delegation of delinquent bikers, so crowded that three were al fresco, perched on the truck's loading bay behind the cabin, brandishing an assortment of weapons. A baseball bat, hunting knife and a wicked-looking motorbike chain. All of which seemed rather excessive, in the scheme of things.

Reaching the exit, Cassidy slammed his foot on the throttle, speeding off the highway, leaving Claude, who was somewhat stoned, almost carrying on, but managing to chase the Roadtrek hurtling down a winding road. Shots rang out again, as the John Wayne of bikers fired from the window. One bullet slammed into the rear window of the motorhome causing frost-like splinters to spread to the window's edges.

The motorhome veered across the centre line almost colliding with a tree and hedgerow, then veering out of control to the other side of the road before straightening up and limping along, turning right, along a narrow lane, wide enough for the Roadtrek to squeeze through, coming to a stop thirty yards along the way, shadowed on either side by tall blackthorn. Silence prevailed, a soft breeze rustling the spiky bushes.

A few minutes elapsed, then the distinctive, low rumble of the Hummer broke the silence as it entered the lane, stopping a safe distance behind the motorhome. A worried-looking Claude stared through the windshield. Above and behind him, three bikers with the same expression laid down their weapons, the same dreadful thoughts as Claude: what if he's dying? What if he's dead? Please say he's playing possum.

At worst, standing in front of the judge, any loyalty towards Claude would have been abandoned when three quivering voices chorused, 'It was him who murdered the drifter, Judge, with his stolen police gun. We're innocent!'

There was only one way to find out. Claude had an ace card up his sleeve: the hobo, Sancho and his two kilo Chihuahua. If Cassidy was alive, Claude was confident, being shielded by his captives, the drifter would have to lay down his weapon. Otherwise…

Dragging them from the Hummer, Claude marched Sancho by the collar, waving his gun, shouting, 'Hey, you! Come out with your hands up, or else the pooch gets it first, and then the hobo!'

Silence. But then came a low groan from inside the motorhome, the sound of someone in great pain.

'Look, mister,' stuttered the mean-looking biker standing behind the Roadtrek, holding the Mexican tight. 'If you're hurt, it's best you come out quietly. I didn't mean to aim at that window, honest. I was aiming for your tyres. We were chasin' you to reclaim that guitar you stole from me. Pass it through the side window and we'll be on our way,' he offered, struggling to hold on to Sancho who was trying to break free.

When he saw the guitar appearing through the window, Claude relaxed. But then it was dropped between the vehicle and the hedgerow, hitting the Tarmac with a resounding jangle of discordant strings and the sound of wood splintering.

Claude looked furious, 'I meant for you to hand it over you son-of-a-bitch, not throw it out!' he snorted. 'As I said, previously, come out with those hands up, you can't be hurt all that bad playin' a trick like that. You ain't gonna make a fool of me twice.'

The biker, red faced, with a murderous look in his eyes waited for a reaction. Waving his gun in the hobo's terrified face, he screamed, 'If you don't come out by the time I count three, the hobo and the dog dies. I aint kiddin', neither.' he growled. 'Your move mister.'

Claude, sweating, shaking with uncontrollable venom, counted, 'One... Two...'

'Bite heem!' yelled the hobo, thrusting the growling animal at the startled biker, her teeth sinking into his revolver hand. 'Bite heem good!'

As the revolver fell to the ground, the tailgate door of the Roadtrek burst open, Cassidy pointing his shotgun at a stunned Claude.

Wearing his Cuban-inspired bandana and olive tee-shirt, the stance of the rebel Che Guevara, he turned the shotgun on the bikers. 'This here shotgun is as powerful, mean, vicious as any that can be found in the world, it being a pump-action Remington 850 Model, Special Purpose Marine Magnum.' He glared. 'It'll stand up to the elements and any other threat, so don't even think about it. Get my meaning?'

Picking up the Colt 38, he threw it over the hedge, telling Sancho to get behind him, not to step on the glasses he'd discarded charging through the door.

'As for you,' he told Claude. 'Empty your pockets of any money on you. It'll go towards me having to purchase a new window.' Cassidy stuffed 30 dollars into his bandana,

Claude had lost his nerve, but apparently not the plot. Falling to his knees, he wailed, 'We were only practising a little road rage on you,' pointing at his girlfriend standing by the Hummer, 'ain't that so, Mistletoe?'

'I told you not to call me Mistletoe,' she grimaced, turning her back on him, folding her arms, kicking a tyre.

'Nice girlfriend,' said Cassidy. 'You two should get married, live unhappily ever after, spawn some more thievin' bastards. Stop grovelling, get up and stand behind the Hummer. Tell your alter egos to do the same, it'll be for your own safety,' he warned.

Claude quickly did his bidding. Huddled behind the massive vehicle, they stood there, perplexed, scared, sweating under the intense sun.

With a huge sigh of relief, wiping the sweat from his brow, Cassidy sat on the tailgate, his eyes focused on the Hummer and those sheltering behind it. Thank God Claude had been born with limited ingenuity. Instead of firing haphazardly at the tyres, he could have used the muscular Hummer to shunt the motorhome into the Cadillac, causing the mini convoy to stop in its tracks. His revenge fulfilled, he could have driven away from the crippled vehicles, celebrating his achievement, sharing a massive spliff with Miss Mistletoe.

Sancho, crouched behind Cassidy, cuddling his heroic Chihuahua, watching as Cassidy raised the shotgun to his shoulder, took aim, and pumped twice, shredding the Hummer's massive front tyres, exploding under pressure, making the front collapse onto its springs, like Claude falling to his knees earlier. Sancho stood aside, making room for Cassidy to get back in, slamming the door shut, shattering the bullet-splintered window. Sliding behind the steering wheel, he drove hell-for-leather along the lane, seeking the highway.

Sitting next to him, Sancho told how he'd been fast asleep when all hell broke loose as dawn was breaking and Claude charged in waving his gun and collaring him.

'Heem bad man, Cassidy, I tell heem, no harm thee dog. He say, 'You and thee pooch, come weeth us. We catch friend.' Scared he shoot me.'

'I dare say he would have,' said Cassidy, glancing at him. 'You were his insurance.'

It dawned on him that the hobo was wearing glasses, the ones he'd lost leaping from the Roadtrek.

'Give me back my glasses you thieving old kleptomaniac,' he laughed. 'You'd steal your mother's wedding ring!'

'I already do that,' he sighed, scratching his head. 'But she forgeev me every time. She know I no help eet. Before she die, she give eet to keep. She good Madre.'

Solemnly, he gazed through the passenger window. 'Good Madre,' he repeated, nodding his head, sighing, then changing course, asking Cassidy why he obeyed the biker; handing over the guitar.

'Why you geev it to thee peeg?' he frowned. 'Now eet is no good to anyone. Why you drop eet to thee floor? Make no sense, amigo. Now you must tell thee owner, he mucho sad.'

Cassidy didnt look bothered. 'Look behind you, Sancho, there, on the bed.'

'Si, amigo. I see guitar case, but no good without thee guitar. Why you smile. No understand. You crazy?'

Cassidy's enigmatic smile changed into a shiny-toothed grin. 'Let me explain,' he said. 'That guitar, the one that went through window crashing to the ground, happened to be a cheap old Spanish acoustic. Cost me thirty dollars. The expensive one in that case belongs to the kid, a relative of mine.'

He saw the perplexed expression on the hobo's face.

127

'Sancho, old friend I'll explain later.'

They joined the highway again, hoping to catch up with the Cadillac.

Picking up the phone, Cassidy rang Pacer, asking his whereabouts, telling him everything that had happened after he and Belle had hightailed it; himself chased down a country road by lunatic Claude, bullets flying close enough to kill; asking how Pacer's morning had gone.

'Well, a little less interesting I suppose,' replied Pacer, aware that his father's tone of voice was tongue-in-cheek. 'I pushed the Cadillac harder than I should have. I didn't know if that Hummer would catch up with Belle and me, so I hit the throttle for about another 40 miles. She was starting to heat up, I had no option but to slow down. You may catch up, otherwise we can hook up near Graceland. I've got access to its car park, but you're gonna have trouble parking anywhere near.'

Ending the call, Cassidy glanced cautiously at the dozing Mexican. 'Wake up, Sancho.'

'Que?'

'Er... I don't know how to explain this to you, without you being offended, but...'

'Que?'

'Well, it's like this,' he coughed. 'Back there, we counted five bikers. Right?'

'Si, amigo,' he yawned. 'Thee hombre Claude, hees woman, and thee three bikers on thee top of thee Hummer.'

'Correct, Sancho,' sniffled Cassidy, turning the air conditioning up full. You were seated behind the driver and his girlfriend, on your own?

'Si, amigo, mucho room for Sancho. Bikers like to feel thee wind on thee face. Why you ask?'

Cassidy leaned out of his window, filling his lungs with fresh air, 'I'll be heading for Nashville after Pacer delivers

128

the Cadillac. Takin' him and Belle with me. If you care to come with us, you'll need to be takin' a shower in that cubicle back there,' he nodded.

The ponging hobo looked baffled. 'Shower? me no comprendo. Sancho no need.'

Cassidy took a second lung-full of air and yelled, 'Sancho! leave the dog and get in that bloody cubicle. Now!'

Dropping the dog, grudgingly leaving his seat, the likeable hobo shuffled to the cubicle grumbling, 'He no understand. Only dirty hombres take shower.'

Ten

BURNING LOVE

It was now almost noon and still no sign of Cassidy rolling up behind the Cadillac, the old girl suffering from heat-stroke, the mechanical kind, as they entered the city suburb, Highway 51. Soon they would be driving along Parkway East, renamed Elvis Presley Boulevard in 1972, that is, if a small leak in her radiator held out until they got there. Escaping from the bikers had meant stopping a number of times along the way, refilling her with the watering can.

Up went the temperature gauge again, causing Pacer to pull in on the side of the busy road. The Fleetwood seemed to be suffering from long-distance fatigue. The past few days had been heavy on her and she was feeling the strain, looking drained, not only being short on water but from her injuries, the broken trunk, the smashed window, kamikaze flies splattered on her windshield, road grime, and topping it all, high fever, steam hissing from her hood.

Nothing could be done, other than for her to cool down again and get the can out, with just about enough water to reach Graceland. While Pacer and Belle sat there, parked beneath a No Waiting sign on the pavement, a uniformed visitor pulled up behind them, blue lights flashing his presence, blazing on his Ford Interceptor.

'Oh, hell,' groaned Pacer gazing through the interior rear mirror. 'Give him your cutest smile, Belle, you never know, if he's in a good mood he'll give us a break, seeing our position. Oh, shit, he's got his ticket pad with him, hand on his gun holster, swaggering, in for the kill.'

Leaning through the driver's window, the well-fed, stocky traffic cop smiled, his eyes focused not on the driver but on his kittenish passenger with the sultry look, returning his gaze with pouting allurement, demolishing Pacer's 'cutest look'. Belle's flirtatious charm had the desired effect on the cop. Like a temperature gauge rising to the occasion.

Dragging his eyes off her, aware he was on duty, he concentrated on his objectivity. 'You blind, buddy?' he scowled. 'See that sign up there,' pointing at Elvis Presley Boulevard. 'No parking on this stretch of road. Now! show me your driving licence.'

While Pacer fumbled for his licence, Belle leaned over. 'We had to stop, officer,' she pleaded, 'there's a leak in the radiator.'

'Yeah, said Pacer, handing over his licence, 'waiting for her to cool down. Give it some more water, we'll be on our way.'

'On your way?' he smirked 'Well, now, let me guess. Kuala Lumpur?' Standing back, observing the colour of his captive vehicle, he rubbed his fat chin and sighed, 'I reckon on it being Graceland.'

Pacer's phone rang. 'Excuse me, officer.'

'Go right ahead, buddy. Just remember, the longer the call keeping me waiting, more chance you'll receive a ticket.'

It was Henderson's chauffeur on the line, worried. 'Mr Henderson, he have relapse. I speak for him. Where you now? Hurry, he die soon.'

'Oh, God,' groaned Pacer, 'I thought he was... Look, tell him I'm almost there, within spitting distance. Tell him to hang on, I've reached Elvis Presley Boulevard.'

'Si, I tell him, but now he die very soon.'

'Jesus,' cried Pacer. 'Look, I'll send a picture of the road sign saying Elvis Presley Boulevard with the Cadillac next to it. He can't die without knowing...'

'Si, I understand. I pray for him. He good man.'

'So will l, Dino, or getting this far will be for nothing. A waste.' Ending the call, Pacer was almost in tears.

'Bad news, kid?' asked the cop, leaning on the open window, his voice expressing compassion. Whether it would last for long was another thing, having to fine him, execute his sworn duty. 'You from England?' he enquired, aware of the accent. 'I got a sister living there in London.'

'That's where my boyfriend lives,' piped Belle, wrapping her arm around Pacer's shoulder, before he could reply. 'He lives in a place called Hammersmith, west London.'

'You don't say,' chuckled the officer, warming to them. 'I was over there, just a few years ago, visiting. She drives one of those black London taxis. Her patch is near Hammersmith, a railway station called Paddington. It's where she picks up most of her fares.'

All Pacer had on his mind, was getting the photo taken, not listening to small talk, but much to his chagrin, he would have to hang on for a while, unless he came up with an excuse to take a photo of the road sign, send it to Dino, pay the fine and deliver the Cadillac. It would be the perfect ending to a long, successful and fulfilled life. Henderson could rest in peace.

The traffic cop was on a roll. Asking him to quit talking would be like telling a mountain gorilla. Weighing around 20 stone, his uniform almost bursting at the seams, it would have been a really bad move.

'Yeah,' he continued, 'That place called Hammersmith is also on my sister's patch. You can't miss her. The other taxi drivers call her by her nick-name, Big Bertha, but her name is Glendora,' he enthused. 'Like me, she finds it hard to get behind the steering wheel. Those London taxis must sure have plenty of room in them, enough to accommodate my little sister.'

Pacer's foot was thumping hell out of the rubber car mat, such was his frustration. Beads of sweat on his brow, he gripped the steering wheel, white-knuckled.

On and on went the chatterbox, yapping about his offspring. Suddenly, Pacer's face lit up. The cop asked Belle to take a photo of both of them standing next to the Cadillac, so that he could send it to his sister. He then beckoned for the other officer waiting in the police car to come join them. It was all Pacer could have wished for, making sure that Belle included the Elvis Presley Boulevard sign as she took another photo on her own phone.

By now, the Cadillac was cool enough to start her engine. The officer was a changed man, like a civil civilian out of uniform. Beaming, he thrust the ticket back into his top pocket.

'Look, you guys,' he said. 'The least my buddy and me can do for you, seeing the condition of this here Cadillac, we'll follow up behind. Keep you company as far as Graceland. By the way, if you ever meet my sister, say that Chuck's asking about her. Chuck Roundtree. Though, between you and me, the guys down at the station call me Chuck 'Wagon' Roundtree. Can't figure out why,' he sighed, clutching his trouser belt and gun holster, attempting to hoist them above his ample abdomen.

Pacer sent the photo to Dino. The officers collected their phones and returned to their vehicle. Glad of the kind assistance offered, Pacer tried starting the engine. It failed a number of times before it kicked in. A single blast of white smoke billowed from the exhaust but went unnoticed by the singer as he cautiously pulled away, followed by the Interceptor, its hazard lights still blazing. With one eye on the road, the other on the temperature gauge, the Cadillac's speed maintained a steady 20mph. Belle, meanwhile, was tight-lipped and edgy with every second that passed. The same could be said about Pacer. They had good reason.

Travelling less than a quarter of a mile, the temperature gauge suddenly reached terminal velocity, having blown its own gasket! The police car's headlights flashing continuously in his rear mirror, Pacer left a trail of white smoke billowing from the Cadillac's exhaust, almost enveloping the Interceptor. Motorists passing the maimed Fleetwood on the busy dual carriageway craned their necks at the grim-faced driver, grimmer, hearing a grinding noise in the engine. The Interceptor's loudspeaker ordered the Cadillac to turn right into a gap in the sidewalk and stop at the entrance to an alleyway a few yards further on.

Meanwhile, the Interceptor carried on along the Boulevard, siren and lights still operating, having been radioed to a far more serious cry in the city.

Pacer turned the rattling engine off and buried his head in the steering wheel, groaning. The game was up, over, finished. The Cadillac was at death's door, as was her owner. Believing only a miracle would save the day, Henderson's death on hold would be stretching things, depending on how long it would take to fit a new gasket.

'What happened?' asked Belle. 'What was that terrible noise coming from the engine?'

Pacer, his face still interred in the wheel, mumbled, 'The head gasket blew. Don't ask me to explain what that is,' he sighed, 'Let's just say it's part of the engine that's broke, leaking scalding water over the rest of it. Luckily, it didn't reach the spark plugs.'

With volcanic pressure, steam was spurting from under the hood, and Belle was getting scared. 'I think we should get out,' she said, hand groping for the door handle.

Raising his head, insensible to her advice, he yawned, saying, 'Nah, she'll cool off. The damage is done. My one and only father should be coming along. I'll tell him to look out for us. Give him our location,' he said, lethargically. 'Might as well sit here and wait.' Making the call, he gazed out the window, ignoring her.

Belle looked annoyed, losing patience, 'Pull yourself together,' she scolded. 'Stop feeling sorry for yourself. You did your best up until the last minute, so don't go blaming yourself. Let's get outta this thing before it blows up.'

'Okay,' he sighed. 'But don't you think you're getting paranoid?'

'Wait,' she said,' touching her nose, 'There's something burning. That's not steam from the hood. It's thick smoke!'

'Bloody hell!' exploded Pacer sitting bolt upright in the seat. It wasn't only smoke that alarmed him. Belle had obviously never heard of the term, 'No smoke without fire', because there was plenty of it escaping from under the hood. 'Can't you see? The engine's on fire... get out!'

Belle didn't need his advice, she was through the door, faster than a lightning strike! But she hadn't reckoned on losing her balance, ending up on the floor, crying out, having badly sprained her trim ankle.

Pacer dived across the bench seat and helped her to her feet. It was obvious, the poor kid was going nowhere on two feet, yelping when she tried. The fire had now taken hold. Fearing an explosion, the gallant singer swept her into his arms and staggered towards the road, gently resting her down on the sidewalk.

His eyes stinging with smoke, Pacer stood there, his pledge, his obligation to Henderson literally going up in smoke. It was heartbreaking seeing the iconic limousine's immaculate paintwork blistering, bubbling, peeling under the intense heat, her distinctive white-walled tyres unrecognisable, highly-flammable rubber feeding the flames. Within minutes, the dense, billowing smoke snaked high, climbing into the clear-blue sky before dissipating over the city, while in the far distance, the urgent wail of a siren.

By now, a large crowd had gathered on the sidewalk, close to the gap where the Fleetwood had first entered. Meanwhile, anyone daring to get closer to the inferno would have found themselves blistered. Belle nursing her ankle, Pacer next to her daunted, having to explain to Henderson, hanging on to life, the facts of failure.

Seeing how anxious the young couple looked, they were approached by one or two in the crowd, asking if they could be of any assistance, especially seeing Belle's condition.

The kindly gestures were appreciated but did little to ease the singer's sorrow, nor Belle's injury. However, he did recognise two figures making their way through the crowd, one wearing a colourful bandanna, and a Mexican hobo cradling a Chihuahua in his arms.

Cassidy, unaware of what car was enveloped in flames, only seeing Pacer and Belle on the sidewalk, in despair. Gripping his son by the shoulders he blurted, 'Are you two okay? What's happened? Is that the Cadillac on fire?!'

Pacer, finding it hard to speak, stared at the burning wreck, nodding his head, eyes welling up.

'Oh, hell,' groaned Cassidy, hugging his son. 'Thank God, you and Belle are okay.' Leaning back, he said, 'Come on, let's get you both away from here, back to the motorhome. Its parked up on the kerb. You've seen enough'

Pacer, finding his voice, 'But Belle can't walk, she's busted her ankle, we'll have to carry her there, between us...' Pointing at the billowing clouds of smoke rising from the Cadillac, he cried out, 'There in the smoke!'

Eyes turned skywards. Cassidy's, Belle's, Sancho's, the Chihuahua's. But all they perceived was billowing smoke.

'Jesus Christ!' he exclaimed 'I don't believe it. Look! Willard Henderson, he's looking down! His face is looking down at us. Can't you see?!'

The apparition must have only lasted for seconds. Looking as if he had just seen a ghost, he turned, seeking confirmation from the others, but there was none, just blank expressions on each face.

Suddenly, in spite of all the commotion the fire had attracted, he had managed to hear his phone breaking through. It was Dino, his voice trembling as he spoke. 'Pacer, have bad news. Mr Henderson, he die. I phone you immediately. You first to know.'

Pacer's day had been arduous, to say the least. Cassidy his father; chased by bikers; confronted by traffic cops; Cadillac in flames; and now this...

'I'm so sorry, Dino. Although we all knew it was about to happen, it's still upsetting, especially for you and Tanya.' He heard sobbing in the background.

'Mr Henderson, he was good boss,' said his loyal chauffeur. 'He treat me like friend for 20 years, after his wife die in accident.'

'That was because you saved his life, wasn't it? Tell me, Dino. Did he see the photo I sent you? The Cadillac parked on Elvis Presley Boulevard.'

'Si, Pacer, he look, he say, 'Good. That will do.' Then he smile, close his eyes. I think he sleep, but he no wake up again.'

Pacer gave a sigh of relief, knowing his dying wish had been honoured. He could now meet up with Elvis, ask for his forgiveness.

Distracted by Cassidy, pointing at the fire engine pulling up behind the parked motorhome with just enough room for the firefighters to get to work, unravelling their hoses. A police car had also arrived. Quickly ending the phone call, he and Cassidy lifted Belle off the floor. 'Make out you're in more pain than you are,' said Cassidy, 'Go to town or they'll have me for obstructing a bloody fire-engine.'

Reaching the back of the motorhome after getting tangled up in one of the hoses, Cassidy left Belle standing on one leg, coughing, spluttering, groaning, crying out in agony, with Pacer holding on to her, looking profoundly distressed.

Leaping into the driver's seat, he drove the motorhome a number of yards further along the road, no longer obstructing the emergency workers. Meanwhile, two traffic cops had arrived, helping carry Belle into the Roadtrek's rear door and onto a bed.

By sheer coincidence, the cops happened to be Chuckwagon Roundtree and his partner. Cassidy re-appeared and Roundtree confronted him with his well-worn phrase, 'You blind or somethin'?' shouting above the chaos.

Pacer quickly intruded, 'Go easy on him, Chuck.' he pleaded. 'This man stopped and offered to take my girlfriend to hospital. You can see she's suffering from smoke inhalation and a broken leg. We have to get her there. Listen to her, she's in a bad way!'

'Okay,' said the huge officer, standing back. 'Get going, but we can't escort you this time round, fella. We gotta move this crowd away from what's left of that Cadillac. Wasn't fit to be on the road, anyway. Should've been in a goddamn museum,' he grunted, spitting at the floor.

The officers turned to leave, Chuck looking suspiciously at the ragged-looking Mexican and his dog. 'You part of this?' he enquired. 'If not, move on old buddy. Wait, give me your name.'

'Why you want name?' grumbled the hobo. 'Me cause no trouble officer.'

'Oh yeah?' enthused Roundtree, gloating. 'How about loitering with intent, under suspicion of being an arsonist.'

'Arsonist? Me no arsonist officer. You make beeg mistake.

Only like Spanish senoritas.'

His vindictive nature towards all vagrants, beggars, bums, caused discomfort to his fellow officer. Chipping in, he asked, 'So, what's your name? Then you can go. You do have a name, don't you?'

'My name? Si, I have name,' came the proud reply. 'Sancho,' he grinned. My mother, she give me good name. Strong name,' sticking his chest out. 'My amigo, Cassidy, here, sometime he call me other name ... kleptomaniac.'

'Let's go!' stormed Roundtree, 'before I bust another button! My day's been bad enough already!'

Mumbling expletives, he cleared off to disperse the ever evolving crowd. With everyone safely inside the motorhome, Cassidy steered the Roadtrek off the kerb. They passed the gates of Graceland where hundreds of fans were already congregating. Within 24 hours, thousands would be on Elvis Presley Boulevard. Who said The King was dead?

With Pacer in the passenger seat, Belle and Sancho lounging behind them, none seemed unhappy to be leaving the turbulent scene. Cassidy accused of obstruction; Sancho accused of being an arsonist; Belle almost accused of playing dead by cynical cops. What next?

Timeworn, deep in their own thoughts, Pacer was first to speak. Turning in his seat, he asked Belle, 'Are you sure you didn't see Henderson's face in that smoke? Please say it wasn't my imagination.'

'Put it this way,' she said, leaning forward. 'I've looked at clouds in the sky and they seemed to be making shapes of things, including faces. A cloud of smoke slowly billowing can do much the same thing, Pacer,' she sighed. 'Another thing, I've never seen Mr Henderson. Not even a photo. I wouldn't know what to look for.'

Pacer wasn't about to give up. 'What about you, Sancho. Did you see what I saw up there? I saw you looking up.'

The hobo gave a wry smile and addressed his dog. 'Hey, Conchita, I theenk you see face in thee cloud. When I look up, I see notheeng only thee smoke, but thee dog, she howl like thee wolf howl. Maybe she see.'

'Yeah,' said Pacer. 'You could be right. Dogs have a sixth sense, that's why she howled, it must have spooked her.'

The beguiling old hobo shrugged his shoulders. 'I theenk, yes, amigo. Conchita, she clever. She have thee seventh and thee seexth,' he praised. 'Maybe thee pink Cadillac, she burn same time as amigo die. She weesh to go weeth heem to thee land in thee sky.'

Tears sprang in the singer's eyes, convincing him into really believing he saw Willard Henderson's visage, timed exactly with the chauffeur's sorrowful phone call.

'Thanks Sancho,' he sighed, grateful for his simplistic, yet spiritual opinion. It made sense to him.

Cassidy had heard quite enough about death. Time to change the record. 'The jewellery in that secret compartment. What are we gonna do about them? They'd be worth a pretty penny in today's market. What about us goin' back?'

'Forget it,' said Belle. 'No way, José. Sorry Sancho, just a figure of speech.' Like most females, having an affinity with jewellery, she knew what she was talking about. 'Diamonds are carbon, just like coal. They take more heat to burn. Everything would be ruined. Only the diamond's core would be left.'

'Okay,' said Cassidy. 'You've convinced me.'

'Look,' she said, sweeping her hair back from her face. 'That Cadillac has held onto the jewellery for sixty years. Like any other girl, she'll want to hang onto it forever. Just keep driving, Cassidy. And if you don't mind, stop at the next drugstore. My ankle needs strapping up.'

'Sure thing Belle. Let's get you sorted with some painkillers as well and we'll be on our way.'

'On our way?' What do you mean by that? A mystery tour?'

'Where do you think?' chuckled Cassidy. 'We're on our way to Nashville, girl.'

Waiting for some kind of reaction from anyone, all Cassidy heard was silence. No protests. 'Okay,' he smiled, turning on the radio. 'Let's hear some music. I reckon we could do with some cheering up.' Tuning in, the first thing they heard was a DJ talking about the weather.

'It's 83 degrees here in Memphis. Sunshine all the way, celebrating a special anniversary that come rain or shine, would make no difference to the thousands of fans expected to arrive tomorrow, and for the lucky ones gathered outside the gates of Graceland, for Elvis's 45th Anniversary. I know it sure is hot out there but nothing like the heatwave of '56, the year Elvis presented the iconic Pink Cadillac to Gladys, his mother. Anyway, folks, let's hot things up a little more with 'Burning Love'.'

'There you go,' said Cassidy, all serious. 'That there song is either coincidence or...'

'Yes, we know!' chorused the others. 'Or it was God talking!!' The motorhome rang with laughter ... all the way to Nashville.

THE END
HOPE YOU ENJOYED THE RIDE!
LONG LIVE THE KING

ACKNOWLEDGEMENTS

I've had a great time writing this book, but it wouldn't have come to fruition without the help of many people. I'd like to thank in particular my publishers, John Kaufman and David Landau, Bob Kelly for the cover design, Simon Hicks for typesetting, and above all, my daughter Tara, my go-between and tech support. Special thanks to Kathryn Krohn for the additional proof reading. And of course, thanks to Elvis, without whom...